I Remember

A MYSTERY NOVEL

Matthew Markland

Archway Publishing books may be ordered through booksellers or by contacting:

Archway Publishing
1663 Liberty Drive
Bloomington, IN 47403
www.archwaypublishing.com
844-669-3957

ISBN: 978-1-6657-3614-5 (sc)
ISBN: 978-1-6657-3612-1 (hc)
ISBN: 978-1-6657-3613-8 (e)

Library of Congress Control Number: 2022924022

Print information available on the last page.

Archway Publishing rev. date: 01/03/2023

ACKNOWLEDGEMENTS

For Austin,

Thank you for always being patient with me and encouraging me to be the best possible me that I could be.

I love you.

CHAPTER 1

I remember. I remember being in this exact place. I remember the feel of the breeze on my face, the calm rustle of leaves floating across the lawn, and I remember the cold nipping at my nose and ears. What I remember most, though, is the pain. I remember the dark and empty feeling that followed. I just don't remember why it happened. And I don't remember when. All I know is I've been here before.

More importantly, I remember him. Yes, the memories of how much love I had for him and the heartbreak that tagged along with his charm I remember all too fondly. But how is this possible? I've only been with him a few years, but it feels as though I've known him my whole life.

Maybe it's some cloudy memory of a movie, or maybe it's my conscious looking out for me. Yet, I love him and hate him at the same time and I cannot fathom how or why on Earth I'm feeling this way. As I continue walking next to him, my mind wanders farther and farther away.

"Are you okay?" Sam's concern shows clearly on his face for my wellbeing. I don't want his sympathy- I want answers. I want to know why I'm having trouble finding my breath and at the same time breathing heavier and heavier. "Leo? Are you okay?"

Snapping out of it, I answer, "Yeah, sorry. I'm just having a bit of déjà vu."

"What of?" He asks, probably whole-heartedly, but his presence this very instance is bothersome.

"I feel like I've been here before and with you, but it wasn't you. Not exactly, anyway. Does that even make sense?" I realize I probably sound bat shit crazy when I ask.

"Well we've been here like a hundred times. It's two blocks from our apartment, so..." He looks at me with a puzzled look and raises his left eyebrow in question- the same face he makes that sets me off lately. I used to think it was cute, but now it just boils my blood. The park we're walking in is only a couple of blocks from the apartment we currently live in. We've been there for almost two years. He told me it'd be temporary until he can get us a house of our own. His empty promises reverberate around the inside of my head so constantly that I'm numb to hope of us lasting much longer.

Rolling my eyes, I start walking faster to put some distance between us. "Why'd you ask if you don't like my answer, Sam?"

"Leo, you're right. I'm sorry. I didn't mean for it to sound like-"

"Like it was coming from an asshole?" I hiss the words before I even have time to think of them.

"What's your problem today? You're acting like a dick for no reason and treating me like crap. I don't have to take this from you, you know. I was fine all morning until I decided to walk home with you. Then it was like this huge, black cloud started following you around."

"My problem is your condescending tone and that awful fucking eyebrow raise you do when you look at me like I'm stupid. I think-" I take a deep breath and slowly let it out trying to alleviate my racing heart. "I think we should take a break. I'm not happy lately and we fight more and more every day. You deserve better and I'm not it."

Sam looks at me in shock at first and walks away. He stands a few feet in front of me, staring off into the distance.

"Sam?" I say, worried at his response.

Letting out a dry laugh, he puts both his hands on his hips and turns around to face me, "Finally."

"Finally?" I repeat his singular, iron-clad word that suddenly weighs heavier on my chest.

"Finally." The smile leaves his face so fast, I barely have time to prepare for what happens next.

Running towards me, he grabs my shoulders hard and throws me to the sidewalk. The concrete, normally cold to the touch, is canceled out by the hot pain my hands are feeling. I lift my palms to see little craters imprinted by the force of them meeting the sidewalk. Quickly they start to itch and I turn my head to look up at Sam as he grabs the hair on the top of my head, pulling it back. Before I can let out a scream, he pulls back and slams his fist down on my jaw.

As I keel forward and spit up a mouthful of blood and what I'm sure is a piece of one of my teeth, he kicks me in the stomach and suddenly the pain in my jaw is muted by the sudden contractions I'm having in my lower abdomen. I throw up blood and lunch and wipe my mouth with my sleeve, unaware if my attacker is still near or not.

Sure enough, before I can pick myself up off the ground, I feel the hood of my jacket get pulled and I'm being dragged across the sidewalk into the damp, lightly frosted grass through shallow mud puddles until all I see are trees and shrubs surrounding us.

"Sam! Please, stop!" I beg as I throw my hands over my face attempting to block whatever attack comes next.

Instead, I feel a very sharp, hot feeling in my side. I let out a shriek as I look down and see a knife being pulled from my midsection and thrust back into my stomach, then back out and then back in, all the while he's saying though gritted teeth, "Shut the fuck up!"

Accepting my fate, I start to pass out, but not before I hear a woman shouting from not so far away. It must have startled Sam, because he ripped the knife from my stomach, wiped it on my now ripped and muddy jeans, whispered something in my ear, and ran.

Fading in an out of consciousness every few seconds, I see the woman whom I assume scared my attacker along with another woman and a man running through the fallen leaves and dodging the dormant trees to get to me as quickly as possible.

"It's going to be okay, sweetie! Help!" She tries to stay calm, but you can hear the panic in her voice. "Reggie, call 9-1-1! Did anyone see which way he went?"

"There's so much blood! What the fuck!" The other woman seems in shock. Debbie- I think I heard the first woman say. "Is he going to make it?"

At this point, I think to myself, I wouldn't bet on it. I want to sleep. It's so cold that my blood seems hot as it soaks the sweater under my jacket and trickles down both of my sides. My eyelids feel so heavy, it's hard to keep my eyes open fully, if at all.

"Hang in there, hon! Help is coming! Stay with us. Just keep listening to my voice." Her panicky voice seems to have calmed down slightly as she realizes I'm in and out of consciousness. "I'm Julie. What's your name?

Annoyed and in tremendous pain, I muster out a dry, "Leo." If that's even my name. Up until a few minutes ago, I was sure I knew all the small details of my life. But now, it's all so distant. What I can't seem to wrap my head around is that this all feels like it happened before. Even the pain feels like a memory.

"Leo, who was that man? Do you know who he was?" Julie asks, trying desperately to hold back the shakiness to her voice. "What did he want with you?"

My boyfriend. It's my boyfriend. We live not far from here. I don't know why he did this! I realize I'm not even speaking as the sounds of sirens in the distance get louder and louder until I can see the flashing lights from behind my almost shut eyelids.

"Sam. His name- it's Sam. He's my-"

What he whispered to me before he ran echoes in my head as the sounds of footsteps rush to help me. 'I'll see you in the next.' I close my eyes and the cold consumes me until I feel nothing.

CHAPTER 2

"No!" I yell as I sit up in bed. What an awful dream. I haven't had night terrors since I was a child and even then they weren't nearly as vivid as this one was. I've never been murdered in a dream before. It felt so real as if I were actually there. Looking down, I notice my sheets are damp from sweating so profusely. I take note of my whole body glistening in the morning sun as I try to slow my breathing. Lying flat in bed, I notice my eyes getting heavy again.

A knock on my bedroom door startles me, "Yes?"

"Evan, it's quarter to ten. You've slept in all morning and your mother is a little more irritable than usual." Lydia says as she opens the door.

Lydia Greene is my family's housemaid, my best friend, and someone I've been infatuated with for the last couple of years as we both have been developing as young adults. She's a little older than I am and started working for my family when she was thirteen and I was eleven. Instantly, we connected. I think the close age helped, but mostly it's because we've come from similar backgrounds.

Like Lydia, I was adopted by a loving couple in New York. The orphanage didn't have a record of my biological parents. Only a note that said, "take care of him- he's our deepest love and greatest pride." Oh, the irony. Why keep one's deepest love and greatest pride close when you can leave them on a doorstep in the middle of the night with a note that screams, "he's your problem now"?

As luck would have it, my adoptive mother and father are extremely wealthy and hold societal power so great that they are regularly looking over their shoulders for the next person trying to take advantage of their wealth. Lydia's family, however, is extremely poor. Mr. and Mrs. Greene begged my parents to allow Lydia to work for the family until her dowry could be established and she could be married off to whomever was willing to marry a peasant girl.

Different circumstances brought us together and a bond happened to form from the same pain of being unwanted by our biological parents. Even now, as I lay in bed staring at her beautiful auburn hair pulled back in a tight ball, I can't help but to smile as I look her up and down with yearning eyes.

"Oh my, I didn't realize you were still in bed, Evan. Shall I come back in a few moments?" Her eyes wandered over the mess of sheets and bulky blanket that lay wildly across the bed and my lower half.

Just as I had gotten my heartbeat to a more stable pace, it started to race again as Lydia closed the door behind her and started walking across the room toward me. We didn't break eye contact. I've been attracted to her for so long I can't help myself around her and based off her climbing into bed beside me, I can tell she feels the same.

I pull her as close to me as I can, feeling her warmth. I lean my face close to hers and deeply kiss her as I start to untie her corset and remove her blouse. She starts to remove the blanket from around my waist and I lay back as she straddles me, lifting her skirt.

A knocking on my door jolts me out of my sleep and I notice I'm sucking on the corner of one of my pillows. Disappointedly, I toss the damp thing to the floor and lay in bed defeated.

"Evan, are you awake?" My father says from behind the closed door.

"Yes, Father. I'm awake," I say curtly. "Come in."

"Great, Son. Lydia is finishing breakfast. Meet your mother and I in the garden as soon as you're ready. We'd like to discuss some things with you."

That's never good. Why must my parents heighten my anxiety first thing in the morning? "I'll meet you in about fifteen minutes."

My father grins, "Make it ten."

As the door shuts behind him, I realize I'm left with a problem I must take care of before any other unwelcome guests make their way to my bedroom-Lydia not included.

I make my way down the stairs and into the foyer quickly, noticing that I'd taken longer than promised and almost run in to Lydia carrying the sterling silver platter out to the garden. Swerving around her, I manage to trip myself on a ruffle of the large Oriental rug in the center of the foyer and fall abruptly on my side which seems more tender than usual.

Strange, I think to myself.

Gasping, Lydia sets the platter on the table in the center of the room and rushes to my side where we both erupt with laughter after she asks, "Are you alright?"

"I'm fine! Really. Just a bit of a misstep." Wiping a tear from the corner of my eye. "How's the tray of food and tea? Mother would have my head if I caused her morning tea to tip."

"The tray is just fine. I'm a lot sturdier than you think, Evan. Even if you had run into me, it'd be as if you ran into a wall," she jokes. "Unlike you, of course. You're built like a straw house!"

"Am not!" I laugh as I push her over and tickle her waist.

Our laughing slowly fades into both of us staring

at each other, yearning for one another in ways that we used to a couple of years ago. Lydia is the reason I'm no longer a virgin after all. Two years earlier, we had chased each other through the garden after her chores and confessed our interest in one another. Shortly after that, a budding romance had started and led to sneaking off into the garden at night to hold hands and kiss in the privacy of the trees.

Eventually, a romance had fully bloomed and the rest is history as they say. It all had come to a grinding halt, however, as my father found out when he watched us scurry across the grounds late one evening from his bedroom window.

"Evan- this must end! What would your mother think of you falling in love with the help? And Lydia- need I remind you that you work for this family? I will not have my only son running off with those under my employment. We must never mix business with pleasure, nor shall we ever speak of this again." I remember him saying. And so we stopped, scared that we had been caught and scared of losing each other forever.

What feels like hours of staring into those beautiful green eyes quickly dissipates as I realize yet again that I'm already running behind on meeting my parents in the garden. I hoist myself off the floor and hold my hand out to help Lydia to her feet.

"I can manage. You mustn't keep your parents waiting any longer." She breaks eye contact and looks down at the floor, smoothing the wrinkles in her uniform.

"Lydia, I-"

"Evan, please. Don't let me keep you."

The longing hasn't left. I still dream about her vividly, as I'm sure she does about me. "Life is about moving forward- never looking back," my father would say. Still, it hurts. I long for a day when status no longer dictates love.

"Let me get the door for you." I skip over to the giant wooden doors at the front of the foyer and open them wide for Lydia to walk through first. "After you, miss."

"What a gentleman!" She smiles, lifting the silver platter and walking through the threshold toward my parents who seem awfully patient for wasps.

"Good morning, my child!" My mother calls across the yard. "Did you sleep well, darling?"

"Now, Olivia, our son needs no coddling. He is, after all, going to be eighteen in a few days," My father responds before I have the chance to.

"Oh hush, Thomas. He will forever be our boy- even when he's started a family of his own." She says after rolling her eyes at my father's remark.

Chuckling, I lean in to kiss my mother's cheek as is customary each morning, "Good morning, Mother. I apologize for my timing- I was getting ready." I blush, knowing that my definition of getting ready differs from that of both my parents. My mind flashes to my first dream that caused me to wake up abruptly. "I did, however, have a nightmare that woke me up in a sweat this morning. It felt as if it were really happening and the strangest part of it all is that I'm sore from it."

"That's certainly puzzling, darling. What happened?" My mother asks, inquisitively. "I can't imagine what would cause you to feel sore after a dream."

"It may be strange, but in my dream, I had been murdered- only it wasn't me and I don't recognize the place I was in nor the clothing I was wearing. It all seemed a bit off."

"Oh my- that certainly does sound strange. And the soreness?" My mother's shock is clearly shown on her face.

"My sides and stomach are sore where I had been stabbed in my dream. It's as if it were actually happening." Aware of how absurd my words were, I decided to move past the conversation and focus on the breakfast being served in front of us. "This all looks exquisite, Lydia, thank you!"

"Indeed. Thank you, Lydia," my father says, nonchalantly ending the previous conversation as well. "As always, you're certainly welcome to enjoy breakfast with us," he says with a hint of reluctance.

"Oh, I couldn't possibly, Mr. Williams. I've so many chores to tend to. Perhaps next time." It was always next time. It's never felt normal since my father caught us.

Unbothered, my father sips his tea and nods his head. "Next time, then."

Lydia empties the tray and scurries off back to the house to continue her daily chores. All the while, watching her walk away leaves my mind wandering. I make eye contact with my father who had been watching me all but drool over God's gift to mankind. I clear my throat, unfold my napkin, and set it in my lap. I smile at both my parents and start to eat my breakfast.

After a quaint meal of poached eggs, rye bread with fig jam, and cups overflowing with tea, my father stiffens in his chair. "Now, for the matter at hand, Son."

"Yes, Father?" I say, swallowing the last bite of my breakfast, which seems harder to get down all of a sudden.

"You will be eighteen in just a few days. That being said, we must look at all options to keep the family legacy alive. Being our only child, we look to you to continue the family name."

My mother continues, "And so, we have arranged for a meeting with a very eligible bachelorette from the city on your birthday!" Her excited tone clearly forced.

"Mother, Father, I appreciate the thought, but I'm not interested in an arranged relationship. I want to find someone who I can learn to love on my own terms. Someone like-"

"Someone like Lydia? There is a greater chance in pigs flying, Son. I told you once and I will tell you one last time. There will be no mixing with the help."

"Evan, I think what your father means to say is-"

"Olivia- I said what I meant. I mean it no other

way." My father says assertively, which quiets my mother. "He is but a boy who is becoming a man. I will not have a man suffer through life based off the decisions he made as a boy. You may think me cruel, Son, but I care only for the future of the Williams name. You'll thank me one day."

Biting my tongue, I know arguing with my father would prove nothing. I would stand a better chance of winning an argument against a bear trap than I would my father. It would probably be less painful, too.

"What say you, Son? Ready to meet the future mother of your children?"

"As ready as I'll ever be, Father." I muster up a smile from the pits of my achey stomach and place my napkin on the table. "May I be excused? I'm not feeling well."

My mother smiles an apologetic one, "Of course, darling. Rest and perhaps you'll feel better later."

As I'm walking away, I can barely hear the quiet argument my parents are having behind me as I hear my heartbeat in my eardrums. Ba-doom. Ba-doom. Ba-doom.

CHAPTER 3

I turn eighteen tomorrow. All I can think about is the conversation I had with my parents over breakfast two mornings ago. My mother has apologized for my father's words multiple times since then, but it isn't her fault. He's the one that's making me meet my "future wife" tomorrow. Mother only goes along with him because she has to. I can't blame her for his actions.

No, indeed it's just my father that's to blame. His word is law here. Little gets past him without his approval. He's not a bad father. He's always been kind to my mother and me. He's just stubborn sometimes and other people have to suffer for it.

I lay awake in bed because I don't want sleep to rush me into tomorrow. I want to keep my life how it is for as long as I can at least for just one more night.

I can't help but to think of Lydia in all this. She's

always been a best friend to me. Always been there when I needed her. I could really use the conversation. If not just for conversation, perhaps just to hold someone I actually love one last time.

I sit up in bed and can make out the shapes of furniture in the darkness. I look around for my robe and slippers and find them across the room. Slowly and as quietly as possible, I slip out of bed and make my way to them. It's late and my parents are surely asleep by now. I haven't seen light from under my doorway in at least an hour.

Twisting the knob as slowly as I possibly can, I open the door an inch at a time expanding my view of the hallway outside my bedroom. When I poke my head around the cool, white doorframe, I see no light coming from under my parents' bedroom door either. With a sigh of relief, I pull my door closed with one hand on the still twisted knob and the other on the center of the door as to muffle any vibrating sounds the door may cause when it closes.

I carefully avoid the known creaks in the floorboards as I make my way to the top of the stairs and peer down to make sure there's no one standing at the bottom of the steps looking up at me with a judgmental face that says, "back to bed, you oaf." Why must Lydia's room be downstairs as if she weren't a part of this family? Why must she be treated like a dog that's not allowed on the couch? Or like a bird in a cage?

Making my way through the corridor downstairs, I finally manage to get to Lydia's door and see it cracked open. With my heart racing, I give a little push on her door and see she's nowhere to be found. Her bed is unmade as if she had been asleep already. Perhaps she can't sleep either? If that were the case, then where could she be?

Just as I finish asking myself that question, I hear a creak come from behind me. I spin around so fast that I dizzy myself and try to focus on the shape of a person standing behind me. I exhale deeply as I see Lydia with her hand over her mouth trying to muffle her giggle.

"Dear God, Lydia!" I hiss. "You scared the hell out of me!"

"Well, Evan, what were you doing outside my room?" She whispers back playfully.

Calming myself, I wipe the bead of sweat forming on my forehead. "I couldn't sleep, and I really wanted to come and see you- I needed to."

Playful expression gone, Lydia takes my hand and pulls me into her bedroom, closing the door silently behind her.

"I'm sorry. I don't want to get you in trouble. I just really don't want to be alone right now." I sit on the edge of her bed and sink my face into my palms. "This is all just awful. I'm to be courted off with some random woman tomorrow and who knows what's going to happen?"

Lydia sits next to me and lays her head on my shoulder. "You know, if anyone can handle big change, it's you."

I turn my head to look at her. Noticing the tears forming in my eyes, she places a hand on my cheek.

"Evan, you've got to be strong. Adapt. Try your hardest to be happy. Any girl would be lucky to have you. I know I sure was." Her voice trails off and she looks down at her nightgown.

"I'm so sorry for everything. If I had known-" She grabs the back of my neck and pulls me towards her, locking her lips with mine.

I can't help but to grab her waist and lay her back on the bed. Pulling her onto a pillow, I lay more of my weight down on top of her as I kiss her deeply. In this moment, I forget about my birthday tomorrow. I forget about the courtship and the sadness that came with the news of it.

In this moment, all I can focus on is Lydia. Lydia: the auburn-haired beauty with the bright-green eyes; the woman who has held my heart ever since I gave it to her those couple of years ago. Undressing each other, I can't help but to take in her scent and feel her soft skin against mine. My lips gently glide along her collar bone and finish their journey in the nape of her neck.

Somehow better than I remember, I'm infatuated with her form. Youthful, but strong. Slim, but powerful. Holding myself back, I push off of her and instead lay next to her. I can feel goosebumps form down her arms as I lightly stroke her skin. Pulling her into me, we lay spooning as closely as we can. Naked, vulnerable, and unsure of what's next for us,

I kiss her shoulders and rub my thumb back and forth against her hands in mine.

Eventually I feel her breathing start to slow and I realize she'd fallen asleep. I can't help but to think that this moment should never end. Oh how I'm lost in her essence. Just her very touch is enough to command me to fly to the moon and back.

Try as I might, I can't help but to feel my eyelids getting heavier and heavier with each thought. Soon, I focus on Lydia's breathing and start to match it as to not disturb her and I fall asleep holding the woman who holds my heart.

As I open my eyes, I notice the curtains have been drawn and I realize that the morning sun is shining strongly through the open window. I lay for a few minutes pondering over the night before and I can't help but to smile so wide that my jaw starts to tingle. And then as quick as I fell asleep last night, I sit up in bed in a panic. I'm still in Lydia's room. It's already well into the morning of my eighteenth birthday and surely my parents are looking for me.

I panic as I notice Lydia is gone and I look around the room, taking notice of a piece of parchment on the bedside table- "Evan" it says.

I open the letter with a playful grin and read, "Come find me." Lydia's handwriting is a specific font that I can instantly recognize from years of leaving love letters under each others' doors at night.

I grab my robe from the floor and put my slippers on. I can already hear my parents walking down the hall on their way to the kitchen- probably to set up for the birthday party and courtship today.

Opening up the door, I make sure no one is outside of the now abandoned bedroom and quickly make my way upstairs to my own room as if nothing happened the night before.

Once I'm inside, I scramble to get ready for the day. It isn't long before I hear my mother loudly greet whoever's at the front door. I roll my eyes, realizing that this birthday party is a facade to my betrothal and take that as my sign to speed up. As I make my way past the huge decorative mirror leaning up against the wall, I stop and retrace my steps until I'm standing face to face with myself.

You've got this, Evan. Adapt. Be strong. Lydia's words come flooding back to me and I remember her letter. Grinning like a fool, I straighten my bowtie and start towards my bedroom door. I grab the doorknob and with a deep breath, I walk through the doorway into the next chapter of my life.

CHAPTER 4

Consciousness starting back up, I hear a few different sounds. I hear a door opening and closing quietly. I hear footsteps moving slowly around me. And I hear his voice, vividly, "I'll see you in the next."

Realizing that Sam could still be near me, I open my eyes so fast that the lighting in the room instantly burns my eyes and I throw my hands up to shield my face from the brightness. I notice the mess of tubes attached to my arm and run my fingers across them, unaware of what they're attached to me for.

"Oh my God! You're awake!" I hear a familiar voice shout as I adjust to the light. "Nurse!"

"Where am I?" I manage to mutter. "Where's Sam?"

"You're in the hospital, sweetie. Do you know how you got here?"

"I don't remember-" I say as I sit up in the bed and feel a sharp pain rush throughout my body. "Fuck!"

As the pain starts to vibrate throughout my body, I start to remember just what caused me this pain. I sit back again, still holding my side as if holding the epicenter of the wound will cause it to magically hurt less.

"Where's Sam?" I say, more serious this time. "Where the fuck is he?"

"The important thing is that he's not here, but sweetie- the cops. They still haven't found him. They checked your apartment, and it looks like he left in a hurry."

"Who- who are you?" I say, realizing I've been talking to a stranger.

Calmly, the stranger explains that she's the one who saw the attack. "I'm Julie. Julie Davids."

"Julie, I don't mean to sound like an ass, but why are you here?"

"My friends and I were out walking when we heard shouting. By the time we had traced where the commotion was coming from, we had noticed what looked like an assault in progress. We yelled at him to go away, and it seems to have worked because he ran pretty fast in the opposite direction. Little did we know, he was actually stabbing you. My friend Debbie tried to follow him but lost him in the woods and our friend Reggie called the police. Luckily, they had a squad car only a couple blocks away, so they got there pretty quickly." Julie had tears in her eyes as she spoke softly, replaying the events of my attack. "That was a week ago."

Stunned, I can't help but to think that I've only been here a few hours. "A week? I've been here a whole week?"

Just before Julie can answer, my best friend Arie walks into the room and rushes to my side, "Leo! You're up!" She hugs me hard, causing me to let out a gasp. "Sorry! I didn't mean to squeeze too hard!"

Wincing, I reply, "That's okay. Just tell me what's going on. Where's Sam? Has anyone else come to see me?"

Julie and Arie look at each other with solemn eyes and I take that as I haven't had much company. The only people that have really stuck around me since I'd gotten with Sam have been Arie and my brother, Alex. Neither of my parents have been in the picture since I came out and most of the friends I had never liked Sam. So, being the good boyfriend I was, I chose him over them. Stupid.

"I called Alex, but he didn't answer. I've been here each day since you were admitted, but only for a few hours each day. Work wouldn't let me take off the full time." Arie looked down at her shoes and I could see she felt awful.

"I understand, Arie. Thank you for coming at least." I say, genuinely grateful to have such a good friend. Realizing that Julie was still in the room, I turn my head towards her questioningly. "And please don't take this the wrong way, but why are you still here?"

Smiling softly, Julie says, "I'm honestly not sure. When my friends and I saw you getting attacked, my instinct told me to stay by your side and make sure you were okay. Even as they loaded you into the ambulance, the paramedics were sure you wouldn't last the ride. But I knew. I knew you'd push through. I had faith that you'd pull through. Plus, after the hospital tried again and again to get ahold of your parents with no answer, I wanted there to be someone here for you to wake up to."

For whatever reason, I started crying. Just the idea of someone caring so much about a stranger that they'd pause their own life for a week to make sure they weren't alone made me bawl. I was crying so hard about Julie and Sam and my parents that I couldn't even squeeze out a simple, 'thank you.' I'm sure Julie understood, however, because she immediately walked to my side and held my hand in both of hers.

"We're gonna get him, you know." Arie said. "Sam. We're gonna get that son of a bitch. I don't know how and I don't know when, but one day there'll be a reckoning. And he better watch the fuck out, because I'll kill him myself for hurting you."

After another few days in the hospital, I was moved to a less intensive unit since my injuries were healing rather quickly. The whole time, Julie stayed with me. I learned so much about her in that short amount of time and I could feel the friendship taking root. She was around my age, maybe in her early thirties, so I think it was pretty easy to relate to her.

After I initially woke up, Arie stayed for a few hours before she had to leave for work. Knowing I was in good hands, she hadn't come back to see me in person since she left. She has, however, FaceTimed me each morning before work and each evening before we each fell asleep. Arie has been like a sister to me since high school. She was the first person I came out to and the only one to open her home to me when my parents kicked me out for coming out to them.

"Are you excited?" Julie asks, smiling a big, cheesy smile. I think she's more excited for me to be discharged than I am.

"I can't even begin to explain how excited I am. Just to be able to lay in my own-" My voice trails off as I realize that I have to go back to the apartment I shared with the man who tried to kill me. Terror fills my mind as I start to sweat at the thought of being asleep one night just to wake up to another knife in my side or worse. "I can't. I can't go back there."

"Sweetheart, you don't have to. I have a spare room you can use for as long as you like. Of course, if you need anything from that apartment, I'll be right there with you. The police haven't seen him in over a week. My guess is, Sam fled when he got noticed and hasn't had the balls to come back."

Relieved, but still panicking, I reply, "Thank you. Really, Julie. Thank you. You saved my life, and I can never repay you for everything you've done- all the sacrifices you've made being here with me this whole time."

"Don't think anything of it, Leo. I feel connected to you for some reason, and I can't just shake you off. What kind of a person would that make me?" She smiles as she starts toward my hospital room door. "Now, I'll be right outside. I placed the clothes Arie dropped off on the bedside table. Get yourself dressed and we can go outside for some fresh air and let you stretch your legs."

I nod at her as she closes the door behind her. I turn to look at the clothes Arie brought for me and I chuckle to myself as I unfold them. The bottoms are sweatpants with a cigarette hole burned on the left leg from a time we tried to be badasses. The shirt is a worn, faded Mickey Mouse tee shirt from our high school senior trip to Disney World. And for a final touch of class, the shoes are Under Armour slides to tie together a look of someone who definitely wasn't in the hospital for almost two weeks.

I let out a gasp and clutch my sides as I laugh too hard for my healing stab wounds. Classic Arie Rose. Leaving only the "nicest" apparel for her closest friend. I smile a little too big and notice myself in the bathroom mirror through the open door of the ensuite. Walking through the door, I turn on the lights, giving myself a better look of the shaggy, stubbled reflection staring back at me. I brace my palms on the counter and lean close.

My face seems thinned out from being in the hospital for so long. I rub my jawline and realize that the stubble is quite literally growing on me. I could get used to the masculinity of it. Add a cute beanie and I'd be going full on hipster. Staring back into my own blue eyes, I hardly recognize myself.

Adapt. Be strong, I think to myself.

Whoa. Déjà vu. I shake off a chill and turn to leave the bathroom. I shut off the light as I exit and grab the small backpack holding all of my belongings from the bed. Looking out the window, I can't help but to wonder where Sam went. Will I ever see him again?

No. Stop thinking about him. You're only going to freak yourself out.

I turn around and take a deep breath before grabbing the doorknob to my hospital room. I exhale and open the door towards me with a newfound purpose in life- to make sure I don't take this second chance for granted.

Pulling up to the apartment building I shared with Sam, I couldn't build up the courage to look out of the window of Julie's Lincoln Navigator. I was frozen. I could've sat there in the front seat all day if it hadn't been for Julie grabbing my hand. Turning to look at her, tears welling in my eyes, I let a slight smile bend on my face.

"I'll be right with you, sweetheart. Take all the time you need." Julie said reassuringly.

After a couple of deep breaths, I unlatch my seatbelt and grab the door handle. "I'm ready."

We make our way inside the lobby and enter the first free elevator. Each ding of it skipping floors in my apartment building made my heart beat faster and faster all the way up to floor seven, where Sam and I shared a life just two weeks ago. It's still hard to believe that someone I was ready to marry could flip a switch so quickly and be so evil. You think you know someone and then you don't.

As the elevator doors slide open, I look down the seemingly endless corridor of apartment doors and see our welcome mat at the end on the right. The "Welcome Fall" sign is still hanging on the Christmas wreath hook we hadn't switched out due to either laziness or the fact that until you're directly in front of it, you can't notice the all-black snowflake design so there wasn't a need to.

With a turn of the key in the locking mechanism and a twist of the doorknob, the door opens to a quiet foyer. The only sound coming from the lifeless space is the heat blowing through the ceiling vents. Even with the thermostat set to seventy-two, there's a chill in the air. The building is old and so the windows bleed cold air into the small, one bedroom space we used to share.

Memories flood my head of Christmas mornings and Netflix nights on the couch. A time when the sounds of love and laughter filled the air and made you forget about the small inconveniences of everyday life. Now the silence is deafening. No laughter. No love. Just a heater that never sleeps in this drafty apartment.

"Should we start in the bedroom? Maybe grab some of your clothes and then work our way around the rest of the apartment?" Julie says, waking me from my daydream.

"That sounds good. I have some empty suitcases in the hall closet. Would you mind grabbing them? We can fill those with my clothes and shoes."

"Sure thing, darling. I'll grab those if you want to get started."

Julie has been the most pleasant part of this last week

and a half or so. I've had someone to talk to, someone to cry to, and someone to keep me company all while holding my hand through each procedure I've had since my attack. With her around, it's easy to forget that my attempted murderer is still at large.

Walking through the already open bedroom door, I walk directly to the closet and fold back the cheap louver doors. For once, they don't stick on their tracks and I can feel my eyes watering. I don't have a lot of fight left in me after these last couple of weeks and I've found that even the simplest things working to my advantage have made me sob uncontrollably. These closet doors almost always stick and irritate me each time they do, but with how smoothly they just opened, I'm on track for the waterworks.

I decide to not humiliate myself and get caught crying about a cheap door opening the way it should, so I start grabbing a few hangers at a time and laying them on the bed. After the first few shirts are laid messily on the bed, Julie walks in dragging three suitcases behind her. She picks up the biggest one, lays it on the bed, unzips it, and throws it open before starting on the next one.

I start to fold my shirts neatly and then immediately lose motivation to achieve perfection and start to smash them into the open suitcases one-by-one. Each hanger that I empty gets thrown against the far wall and I grind my teeth with each toss. I can feel my face getting hot as my eyes start to water yet again.

Julie notices and stands beside me patiently. "It's going to be okay, Leo. It's going to take some time, but it'll-"

"Fuck him! Why did he do this to me? I can't even open a god damn closet door without wanting to break down and cry! He took everything from me and left me to die!" Sobbing, I drop to my knees and sink my head into the mattress before me. "I wish he just killed me when he had the chance. This isn't a life. I'm scared every single day and I'm just waiting for him to walk through that door and finish what he started."

"Oh, Leo. I'm so sorry, love. I can't begin to understand how you're feeling right now. I don't know if I ever will. But let me tell you something right now." She kneels beside me and grabs my face in both her hands, turning my head in her direction. "You don't have to go through this alone. Do you understand me? You have me here with you and I'm not going anywhere."

I wrap my arms around her and she cradles me like a child as we both cry in silence, only to let out a sniffle here and there. "Thank you," is all I can manage to squeak out in between gasps.

After a few hours of cleaning out my stuff from the apartment, we finally finish loading the Navigator and I leave my key on the counter of the now almost-empty apartment. Without turning back, I walk out, closing the door behind me. Julie stood by the elevator while waiting for me to finish up.

"You hungry?" She asks as her stomach loudly rumbles.

"I could eat. What did you have in mind?"

Shrugging her shoulders, "Something greasy. Maybe a burger. What's good around here?"

"There's this diner a few blocks away. Arie and I would go there every time we went out drinking. It has probably the worst service, but best food I've ever had."

"Sounds like a winner to me!"

The elevator doors open with perfect timing and my mouth starts to water thinking about food. I haven't had actual food in almost two weeks and I'm starting to forget what non-hospital food tastes like. If I see another fucking pudding cup I might hurl.

The waitress brings the check to our booth without as much as a smile and says curtly, "Whenever you're ready," before walking back to the checkout counter.

"What if I wanted dessert?" Julie whispers sassily to me.

I'm guessing we both laugh harder than we should of

because the waitress shoots us a look so dirty, it could've made the paint peel from the walls. Seeing her expression only makes us laugh harder before we crawl out of the booth with our jackets in hand. Julie hands me her keys and asks me to start the car while she pays.

Walking out to the car, I'm reminded how cold it's getting and decide it's best to put my jacket on before crossing the parking lot. Stopping at the bench outside to put it on, I get a weird feeling of being watched. I start to look around quickly and see no one outside. I start visually scanning the cars in the parking lot for any signs of life before I feel a hand grab my shoulder.

Turning around quickly, I notice it's just Julie and feel instant relief. "God. I thought you were someone else."

"Oh my goodness, I'm so sorry. I was going to ask if everything was okay. You were just standing here frozen and I didn't know if you'd seen a ghost or not."

"Not a ghost- just felt like I was being watched." Noticing how paranoid I was starting to sound, I handed her back her keys and started to cross the parking lot before making sure no one was coming.

"Leo, look out!" Julie shouted as a car skidded to a stop, nearly colliding with me in the crosswalk.

I stopped in my tracks, frozen in place as I looked through the windshield to see who almost flattened me. The windows were tinted, so there wasn't a lot of light in the car to help make out the face of the driver, who was wearing sunglasses on this otherwise gloomy day. Before I could get a good look at whoever he or she was that was driving, Julie grabbed my arm and pulled me past the front of the car towards her parking spot.

Flipping the driver off, Julie turns to me, "Do me a favor? Could you please, please, please look both ways before you cross the street? You just got out of the hospital- do you really wanna go back? Because I'll tell you one thing- I can't do another two weeks sleeping in that cheap recliner."

"Sorry, I'll look out next time." Feeling like I had just be scolded by my mother, I walked behind her to the car like a dog with its tail between its legs.

Buckling our seatbelts, Julie turns to me, "I'm sorry. I didn't mean to snap at you. Can you believe that asshole? Who drives like that through a parking lot? What if there had been kids?"

"Welcome to New York." I say, chuckling.

CHAPTER 5

Looking up at Julie's beautiful home, I can't help but to imagine what she does for work. Her house is a huge, tastefully painted Victorian home with some of the best landscaping I've ever seen. She must be the owner of her own company or some big-wig corporate executive because she's definitely missed work for almost two weeks and that usually doesn't fly well in a normal nine-to-five job.

There's also the all-too-familiar feeling of déjà vu I've been experiencing more frequently as of late. If I close my eyes, I can picture running around on the front porch as a child and being chased through the gardens while my parents call out for supper. When I open my eyes though, I'm back to the present, sitting in Julie's front seat and staring at the house in amazement.

"Your house is gorgeous! You live here all by yourself? How did you find something like this with the market like it is?" Realizing I was sounding a little too excited, I slowed my pace and waited for her to reply, all while staring at her wondrously.

Chuckling, she said, "Well thank you, Leo. I actually inherited this house from my parents and they inherited from my mother's parents and so on. This house has been in my family for generations ever since it was sold to us back in the late 1800s. I think I'm the only one that saw the true potential in it and have tried my hardest to bring it back to life- one small coat of paint at a time."

"Well, you've really outdone yourself. This place looks amazing. I can't wait to see the inside!"

"Right! Let's get you settled in. I'll give you a tour and we can come back for the bags."

Following behind Julie, I'm taking note of each small detail of the exterior from the ornate spindles on the railing to the old-age iron locks on the shutters. Each handcrafted piece of her house has a story it wants to tell and I'm ready to listen.

As soon as the giant front door opens, my jaw all but hits the beautifully restored hardwood floors. Once inside, my eyes are drawn directly up, where a massive gold-colored chandelier hangs from the twenty-something foot ceiling. While distracted by the statement piece and unaware of my new surroundings, I trip on the corner of the central rug and fall disgracefully onto my knees which reopens the scabs that have almost healed completely. Before I have a chance to pick myself up, I'm engulfed by the feeling of déjà vu yet again.

Three times in one day? It seems odd, but it must just be a coincidence.

"Oh dear! Are you okay? I should've warned you about this old rug- there's one corner that has a slight curl in it and no matter what, I can't seem to flatten it out. Must be due to old age. It is almost 200 years old, after all. I'm surprised it's lasted this long," Julie says all while helping me to my feet.

Brushing off my sweatpants, it takes me a second to realize what Julie had just said to me. I was so preoccupied that I almost missed the whole conversation.

"Yeah, I'm fine. I feel like I've been here before, though. Like on this exact rug." I say, aware of how weird I sound. "It that crazy?"

"Oh? Well weirder things have happened, I'm sure. I don't think it's crazy- maybe just a little specific, but I'd also like to think that you haven't been in my home before today!" Julie says with a laugh. "Let's proceed with the rest of the tour, shall we?"

After the rest of the tour, Julie let me pick which room upstairs I'd like to stay in. The one and only bedroom on the first floor was "absolutely hers" she said. I had absolutely no problem with that. I'd rather be as far from the front door as possible just in case a certain unwelcome visitor makes his way into the house after me. I shutter at the thought and make my way up the stairs.

Upstairs has a total of four bedrooms. There are two at the top of the staircase, one across from the other. The third is midway down the hall on the right. At the end of the hall is the fourth bedroom, across from the bathroom. I took the one across from the bathroom just to make my life easier. It just so happened that the room I chose was big and airy with a style that's a little too vintage for my taste, but I can appreciate Julie trying to keep up with the aesthetic of her Victorian home. I can't complain too much, either. She is, after all, allowing me to stay in her home until I can get back on my feet. Quite literally, too, since she just helped me off the floor about an hour ago.

I unpacked my suitcases and stored them under the bed. Looking around the room, I noticed there was no closet- just a large wooden armoire. Working with what I had been given, I hung up as many of my clothes as would fit and stuffed the rest in the dresser across the room.

Yawning for the third time since starting to unpack made me realize that the exhaustion was finally catching up with me. I sat on the bed and was shocked at how comfortable the mattress was. I laid back with my feet hanging over the side and shut my eyes to take in the comfort for just a few measly seconds.

A few hours later, I jolted myself out of my sleep, and noticed that I was in the same position I had fallen asleep in with the lights still on. I reached for my phone and saw the time read: 1:48AM. I set my phone down on the nightstand and decided to take a quick shower to wash the previous day off.

I made my way across the hall and into the full bathroom opposite my bedroom door. Once inside, I shut the door as quietly as I possibly could, all while holding the center of the door to silence the vibrations of the door latching- a habit I picked up quickly after coming home way past bedtime as a teenager.

I turned on the water and waited the few seconds it took to get warm before turning the shower head on. Removing my clothes, I couldn't help but to notice in the mirror the artwork of bruising down the sides of my body like a messy, used canvas. Awful shades of blue and purple with a glow of yellow outlining was enough to ruin any ounce of self confidence I used to have.

Taking off the gauze took the longest because my blood

had crusted it to my skin. Simply "ripping it like a Band-Aid" wasn't going to work here so I slowly, painfully peeled it away from my skin and took note of the damage Sam had caused. Each stitch was a tally mark for how many times I'd hurt him if I ever saw him again- *when* I see him again.

Finally undressed and unwrapped, I stepped into the warm rainfall and braced myself for the pain of the water hitting my sutures. To my surprise, the tingle was milder than I thought it would have been and I stepped forward, fully enveloping myself in the stream of the updated shower head that Julie just couldn't stop talking about. "This is my favorite bathroom in the whole house because of this shower head, right here," she pointed. Cue the long, detailed story about how she came to obtain it and how long it took her to install it. She did good, though. I can certainly attest that it's working perfectly.

I think this is probably the best shower experience I've had in a long time. I can't help but to just stand under the water and let the warmth flow over my achey body. I'm hurting all over, but this feels good. After everything that's happened to me, it's interesting how even just a warm shower can provide even the tiniest glimmer of hope that not all things are bad, I guess.

Almost a half hour later, I turned the water off and reached for my towel. I decided patting myself dry was the best, least painful way to do it. Carefully dabbing my stitched, Chucky the Doll areas, I grabbed some fresh gauze from the first aid kit under the sink and reapplied gratuitously over my wounds. When I was done, I opened the door and tip-toed across the hall into my bedroom and shut the door the same way as I did the bathroom.

Once inside, I removed the towel and looked at myself one more time before going to bed. Take away the gauze and the bruises and I'm pretty hot. The weight lost in the hospital finally shows my abs again and is that a v-line?

I pulled open one of the drawers of the dresser I had just carefully unpacked my clothes into earlier and grabbed a pair of basketball shorts. I decided not to attempt wearing underwear until I'm fully healed- one: because that requires way more work than I'm prepared to take on at the moment and two: please see number one. As if I need an excuse for myself anyway. *Eye-roll.*

After climbing into bed, with the lights off, it doesn't take long before I feel my eyelids getting heavy. I start to focus on the sound of the ceiling fan rotating above me and I close my eyes only to fall asleep moments later.

CHAPTER 6

As I awaken, I can hear the sound of the rain falling upon my bedroom window. It almost makes me fall back to sleep before I notice the sounds of footsteps from outside my door pacing back and forth. I lay for just a bit longer, pretending not to have woken up yet so no one knocks on my door. By the sound of the footsteps, I can tell they belong to my father. He's infamously heavy-footed and paces when distressed.

My bride-to-be never arrived at my birthday party over a week ago, where we were supposed to meet. So if anything is stressing my father out, it's the fact that his only child and son is still without a wife of his own. Eventually the footsteps fade as he walks away. I turn onto my back and lay staring at the ceiling; pondering all the reasons she didn't show up as planned.

It's not that I'm not upset that she didn't come- a

bit relieved, actually. After expressing to my father that I'm not ready for marriage and him ending the conversation abruptly, telling me that a man my age should already have a child well on the way, I'm thanking God that I've been spared for a bit longer from such a commitment. It's only a matter of time before he finds another eligible bachelorette for me, but at least for now, I'll bask in my loneliness.

Lost in thought, a knock at the door startles me and I yell, "Come in!"

The door creaks open and Lydia pokes her head in. "Good morning, Evan. How'd you sleep?"

"Fine- a bit warm, but fine, nonetheless. And yourself?"

"Hardly at all, I'm afraid. I kept tossing and turning and couldn't get comfortable for the life of me." She shows a tired smile and yawns. "But duty calls and so I must answer."

"You know, my bed is exceptionally comfortable, if I may say so," I grin. "You're welcome to try it out with me anytime!"

Chuckling, she waves her hands at me and shakes her head. "In your dreams, Romeo."

"Wishful thinking, I'm afraid." I shrug my shoulders and sit up in bed. "You work too hard, why not take a break and rest?" I pat the space next to me on the bed and give her a yearning look.

Starting towards my bed, she stops and looks down at the floor. "No. We can't keep doing this, Evan. My heart can't take it anymore." She turns and starts to leave.

Jumping out of bed, I rush in front of her and stand against the closed door.

"Evan, please get out of the way."

"Lydia, I don't want you to go. I need you to stay. Please."

"But what about-" I grab the back of her head and kiss her firmly. Half-expecting her to pull away or push me off, I'm surprised when she wraps her arms around my neck and shoulders.

I push off of the door and towards the bed, all while still kissing her. Moving toward the bed, I start to untie her apron and unbutton her blouse. When I'm done, I start to slip it off her shoulders and take comfort in her silk-like skin. Kissing down her neck, I start pecking her shoulders with my lips and can hear her breathing quicken.

We stand against one another, kissing and feeling the warmth of each embrace. I lift her small frame and lay her on her back in the spot I just jumped up from. Kissing still, I breathe her scent with each inhale and exhale hungrily with each breath.

In this moment, I have not a care in the world. Lydia is the first and only woman I've laid with and before long, I'm inside of her again- longing for the passion we once had. Heavily breathing in each others' ears, still embracing as tightly as we had just a moment before, I'm imagining a life with her and only her.

Soft moans escape her lips as I hush her with a kiss and continue to thrust into her until we both exhale one final, pleasurable time. It doesn't take long before we go at it again, sharing a moment we both have desperately needed for a very long time.

A few hours after my encounter with Lydia, I'm standing before my mother and father in the parlor of our house. Both of them had witnessed Lydia leaving my room this morning and no amount of denial has proven reliable. Raining harder now, I focus on the sound of it hitting the windows and the sight of the drops racing themselves down the glass instead of my father's agonizing lecture about being with the help.

"Are you listening to me, Son?" My father asks, seemingly annoyed with my lack of attention.

"Yes, Father." I say with a roll of my eyes.

"Then repeat what I said just now." He looks at me with anticipation.

After a few seconds of silence, all of which confirms my ignorance of his aforementioned lecture, he stands, buttoning his suit jacket. "As I said: Lydia must go."

"Father, no! She did nothing wrong!" I say, looking to my mother for defense.

My mother instead sits quietly, staring blankly at her hands, clasped tightly in her lap. She's never been the type to stand up to my father or help change his decision. Mother has always been passive when it came to Father. Always going with what he says just to avoid starting a war.

"Father, please. You're not thinking clearly. If you just let me explain-"

"Explain? What's there to explain? You gave me your word. Both of you did. I told you there'd be consequences for these actions had they presented themselves again. It was the both of you who chose to continue this charade. Mucking about all over the property and under my own roof! There is no discussion. Lydia leaves this evening. Understood? She'll get enough time to pack a trunk full of her belongings and then I'll have the carriage take her home."

"This is her home! She hasn't lived with her family for years!"

"You're out of line, Son. I won't have this disrespect in my home any longer." Holding his palm out in front of me in an act of silencing my words, he starts to walk out of the parlor. I stand in front of him, challenging him with my stance and glaring at him. "Out of the way, Evan. Now."

I stand my ground, only solidifying my feet as to be ready to stop him from pushing past.

My mother stands and rushes in between us. "Enough- both of you! Evan, what has gotten into you?" She turns and looks at me with a disappointed expression.

My father sighs and puts his hands on my mother's shoulders, also looking at me with wondering eyes.

"I love her. She can't go back- they don't love her there." I say, tears welling in my eyes.

My mother takes me in her arms and holds me close. "I know, darling. Love like this is painful, but it's also your first. You'll learn to love again. Trust me."

Just then, Lydia walks into the room holding her jacket in one hand and a closed umbrella in the other. Her eyes are puffy where she had been crying and she sniffles a bit before dabbing a tear from the corner of her eye and straightening her back.

"I'm ready to go, Mr. Williams," she says quietly.

Clearing his throat, my father says, "Right. I'll have the driver take you home. I'll walk you out."

Lydia makes eye contact with me for a split second that feels longer than it was. Was this it? Is this the last time I'd see her? It's all wrong. We're in love. How could Father do this? I start to sob as mother pulls me closer, leaning her head on my shoulder.

Father escorts Lydia to the front door, opens it, and they both walk outside under the umbrella Lydia was carrying. The door shuts behind them and it suddenly feels all too quiet in the house. The only sounds are coming from the rain hitting the parlor windows and the crackle of the fireplace which has now dimmed due to negligence.

I stand up and walk to the window, looking out in time to see Father give Lydia a hug just before he helps her into the carriage and hands her the umbrella. It's raining even harder now and Father still stands just outside the carriage as the driver tugs the reigns, causing the whole thing to jerk forward with the horsepower of two miserable, wet horses. Still, my father stands there- waving at the carriage until it's finally outside of our gates. He turns and starts to walk back to our front door, only to stop when he meets my gaze through the window.

Almost immediately, he looks away and continues walking towards the front door. Before he manages to get to the door, I decide to make myself scarce and head upstairs as quickly as I can while ignoring my mother calling after me. I get to the top of the staircase just in time to hear the door open. I don't look back as I rush down the hall to my bedroom, where I go in and throw the door shut. It slams as I jump into my still-messy bed where I had just an hour ago shared the most amazing two hours with the love of my life.

How could Father do this? Why is it so wrong?

Thoughts keeps racing through my mind as I wonder of the life Lydia will have after leaving this house. Her family was quick to send her away once, what will they do if they get the chance again? My head is aching so violently from overthinking and crying so hard that I hardly notice when I get too comfortable and drift off to sleep.

CHAPTER 7

About a month has gone by since Lydia was made to leave our house. Each day that passes gets a little easier, but my guilt never waivers. I feel like it's all my fault and no matter how many times my mother tells me otherwise, I can't help but to blame myself. If I could see her, I'd tell Lydia how sorry I am and give us both the closure we need. I can't consciously move on until she knows that I never meant for any of this to happen.

While I've been hiding myself away in my bedroom, only to come out for breakfast or dinner, my father has been keeping busy trying to find me a suitor to marry and bare children. It's sickening that he has no remorse and only the ambition for me to carry on the family name with someone he thinks is perfect for me. Am I not a man now? Am I not able and willing to make my own decisions as a man?

Still, he is my father. Granted- he isn't my biological father, but still the only father I've ever known. His word is law and I know deep down inside that he's doing all of this in my best interest. But even so, I cannot lie and say I have no resentment for what he did to Lydia. We could have made it work if she stayed. We both could have promised not to see each other romantically. Couldn't we have?

My mother likes to say that everything happens for a reason, but what reason could it be to tear two people apart so viciously?

"Darling," my mother says as she opens my bedroom door. "Come to the parlor for tea. Your father is out to town and I could use the company."

"I'm not in the mood for tea, Mother. Maybe next time."

"It wasn't a choice, my love. More of a command. Two sugar cubes or three?"

"Two." I say as the door closes quietly. Why can't everyone just leave me alone?

I get out of bed and draw back the curtains. The sunlight fills the room for the first time in weeks and I can't help but to notice the dust swirling through the beams of light coming through the windows. Lydia's been gone almost a full month and coincidentally the dust moved in right after. I haven't the motivation to clean my own room. I haven't the motivation for anything, really.

I grab my robe from the hook on my bedroom door and make my way downstairs to the parlor. On my way down, I overhear my mother speaking to someone- a man. Only, this man is definitely not my father. His voice sounds younger. I slow my pace and wait just around the corner until I hear my mother quiet herself.

"Evan, darling. Come in and introduce yourself." She calls from inside the doorway.

Almost immediately, I come around the corner as to make it seem like I had just come down the stairs and wasn't trying to eavesdrop. I see my mother sitting on the parlor couch, smiling at me as the stranger turns around.

A young man, seemingly not too much older than I am, turns and stands up. He reaches his hand out to shake mine, but I'm encapsulated by his wicked good looks. He's taller than me with dark hair and beautiful, hazel eyes. I realize I'm staring for too long and shake my head as I extend my hand to meet his.

"Evan. Evan Williams," I say, hoping he didn't notice me staring at him like a dog, begging for a biscuit. Certainly, I'm no homosexual. I've only been attracted to women my whole life and the only sins I've committed are those of lust with Lydia. I'm still in hot water for those, so adding a rumor of homosexuality would be the cherry on top. I could kiss my inheritance goodbye and my family, too, for that matter. After all- this is simply just a man thinking another man is attractive. There's nothing wrong with the thought so long as I don't mention it out loud.

Smiling with such an unbelievably perfect smile, the stranger replies, "Benjamin Samuel Crane. Pleased to meet you, Evan." Holding my hand in his for slightly longer than what proves comfortable, his gaze locks onto mine and his smolder makes my heart want to leap out of my chest.

I pull my hand away quickly, flabbergasted at the thoughts running through my head about this strange man in my house.

"Mother, may I ask what Mr. Crane's business is with us this morning?" I ask, desperately trying to move the conversation forward.

"Benjamin here is our new housekeeper." My mother says, sipping her tea.

"A male housekeeper?" I start, "I don't think-"

"I assure you, Mr. Williams, my experience comes from previous employment as a butler's apprentice with the Wilsons in Virginia and the Franks in Massachusetts. I've been taking care of houses for the last five years and I promise to take care of yours. It's my primary duty and I shall cherish it with honor and grace. You need not worry about a thing while I'm here.

"I'm not worried, Mr. Crane. You're just-" Thinking quickly, I try to make up a reason he's unfit, "Younger than I would've imagined."

"Please- call me Benjamin." He says, looking me up and down with wandering eyes. "I'm young, but very experienced."

I stand there, having trouble swallowing while translating his flirtatious comments and staring blankly at the couch behind him. I've never had a man flirt with me this much, let alone so obviously and in front of my mother! How has she not noticed?

"Mother, may I be excused?" I ask, eager to leave the room I'm in at once.

"You may- only after you've shown Benjamin to his quarters. He can have the room down the hall from yours."

"What about Lydia's old room? Can't he just have that one?"

Shaking her head, "No, darling. Lydia's old room is going to face some renovations and be turned into your father's new office at home. He's getting too wary to make the trip to town lately. It's best for him to be here and a more capable young man to make the trips for him."

Defeated, I nod my head and turn to Benjamin, "Right this way, Mr. Crane- Benjamin."

I extend my hand in the direction of the staircase and wait for him to grab his bags and start up the stairs. Following a few stairs behind him, I'm aware that his backside is poking out intentionally as I'm almost eye-level with it. I'm not sure what his angle is, but he is sadly mistaken. Still- it is a lovely backside. I tighten my robe and try to think of something else.

Reaching the top of the stairs, Benjamin stops and marvels at the chandelier hanging just at arm's reach over the foyer. I take the opportunity to walk past his distracted eyes and start down the hallway. It doesn't take long before he realizes I've almost left him and he hurries down the hall behind me.

"I must say, Evan. You're very lucky to live in a house such as this. I've not seen architecture like this before."

"Yes, it's quite remarkable," I say, stopping outside his assigned door. "Here you are. Can I get you anything?"

Pushing the door open, he walks inside and sets his bags down on the floor next to the bed. He sits down on the edge of it and looks up at me. Slowly taking off his gloves, he smolders again at me.

"I can't think of anything you can get me. But when I do, I'll be sure to let you know, Mr. Williams." He winks at me and I pull the door closed abruptly. I hear him let out a quiet chuckle as I head down the hall to my room and shut my door behind me.

Am I imagining this? Am I losing my mind? There's no way Benjamin could be flirting with me. Homosexuality is a sin. No one in their right-mind would risk doing something so vulgar as laying with the same sex… Right?

I shake off the thoughts and pick up the first book I see. I lay in bed and try to focus. Trying to read with my thoughts running circles around me is too difficult so I toss the book to the floor and stare at the ceiling. I lay there for a few minutes before sitting up and looking out the window.

I start to daydream about Lydia throwing open my bedroom door and walking towards me while only wearing her corset. I can't help but to get an erection and close my eyes, trying to envision her kneeling before me, removing my robe and pushing me to lay back on the bed. A few seconds of pleasure go by and I look towards my groin to see Benjamin looking up at me while taking me in his mouth.

I open my eyes quickly and stand up when I notice my throbbing erection in the mirror. Disgusting, I think to myself. What the hell is wrong with you, Evan?

Rolling my eyes, I decide I need fresh air and a walk through the gardens sounds like the best way to obtain it. I get dressed, ignoring the leftover stiffness that has since fallen out of my robe and tuck it into my trousers.

Opening my bedroom door, I peak out to make sure the door diagonal from mine is still closed. When I decide that the coast is clear, I head downstairs, walking quickly through the foyer, ignoring my mother calling my name from the parlor.

After dinner, I decided to share a couple glasses of scotch with my father. While sipping the first glass, my father told me about a couple of different families in town that have daughters my age with ‘the best birthing hips’ he's ever seen. Why on earth my father insists on telling me these things about potential suitors, I'll never know.

Before I even realized, I was pouring another glass for myself and, while holding the crystal decanter, gestured to my father for a refill of his own. He gulped down the last couple of sips from his glass and reached out with it for me to fill.

The second glass went down much more smoothly and I could start to feel the warmth of the first. Like the second glass, the second conversation also went smoother than the first. My father and I talked about hunting and the older days when I was a boy and he'd take me for carriage rides after dark to catch fireflies in the fields not too far from our home.

This is the father that I wish was around more often. Not the father that holds his nose higher than everyone else's and whose status is more important than his son's love. The laughter we're sharing gets locked away lately, only to come out with the good scotch.

My father stood and poured another glass for himself, gesturing this time to me with the decanter. Shaking my head, I finished my second glass and told my father I was off to bed. Nodding, he cheered his glass to my empty one and plopped down on the parlor couch, staring into the flames of the active fireplace.

On my way up the seemingly higher-than-usual staircase, I all but relied on the railing to hold me up the whole climb to the top. I let out a silent cheer when I reached the top all by myself and looked around, hoping no one saw me. I let out a drunken laugh when I verified I was alone.

I made it to my bedroom door and was having trouble with the handle when I heard a voice come from behind me.

"Too much to drink?" Benjamin said.

I spin around and make eye contact with the dimly lit face from inside the open door. He's lying in bed, reading the book I tossed to the floor earlier in my room. From here, I can see he's not wearing a shirt and the blankets are barely covering his lower half- one of his legs sticking out from underneath.

"A little too much I admit." I said with a hiccup. "What are you reading?" I ask, knowing the answer to my question already.

"The book you left on your bedroom floor along with piles of dirty trousers and undergarments." He said with a sly smile. "Won't you come in?"

"I've been meaning to talk to you, so yes. I will come in. On my own accord." I state, pushing the door closed behind me. "What game are you playing?"

"Game? Whatever do you mean, Evan?"

"Don't think me mad, Benjamin. I've seen the way you look at me. And the little flirtatious comments toward me. What is your goal here?"

"My goal? Evan, you sound paranoid- not mad. What exactly are you getting at?"

I sit on the end of the bed, pushing his feet out from beneath me. "Forget it. It's stupid."

Sitting up, Benjamin swings his legs over the side of the bed and sits about a foot away from me with the blanket barely still covering the area between his waist and mid-thighs. The dim light in the room is highlighting his abdomen and muscular chest, doing justice to his form.

"It isn't stupid if it's how you're feeling. I want you to be able to think of me as a friend. You can tell me anything." He looks deep into my eyes and his expression is a longing one.

"It just seems like since I met you this morning, you've had this urge to want to-"

"To fuck?"

Startled, I just look at him with a confirming expression. "Yes."

"Well, I do want to." He scoots closer to me and places one hand on his groin area above the blanket and the other on my thigh. "Really bad." I can see the blanket rising beneath his hand.

I feel myself getting hard, but at the same time I'm confused. I've only ever been with a woman. I've never been attracted to a man before- before Benjamin.

"What are you doing?" I ask as he removes the blanket, exposing his nude body sitting only mere inches from me now.

"I'm doing what I've been wanting to do since I saw you this morning- pleasure you with every ounce of my being." He pushes me back on his bed and removes my undershirt and unbuttons my trousers.

"Wait!" I say, sitting up quickly. "I can't do this."

"Evan, what's stopping you?"

"You're a man, Benjamin! And so am I. It's forbidden. It's sinful. It's-"

"Everywhere in nature. Everywhere. What makes humans any different than animals? Two male lions can fuck each other in the Savannah and everyone thinks it's beautiful. Why can't a man pleasure another man without being called a sinner?"

I fire back, "We're not animals! We are distinguished and we hold ourselves higher than savage beasts. What would happen if my mother found out? Or worse- my father?"

"I won't tell, Evan. It's a secret that I'll take to the grave with me."

Considering the promise he just made, I sit quietly, staring into his lustful eyes and at his full lips that are now pouting. He notices me looking at his mouth and slowly bites his bottom lip. He hasn't lost his erection this entire conversation and he starts to touch himself as he gets closer to me.

"Please, Evan. I promise I won't tell." He kneels before me next to the bed and continues unbuttoning my trousers. "It'll be our little secret." I grab his hands and contemplate leaving again.

Noticing my hesitation, he proceeds with undressing me. I have no desire to stop him, strangely. I think about my daydream earlier in the day and get harder. Benjamin notices too and I suddenly feel the warmth of his mouth on my groin. I close my eyes in pleasure and lay back on the bed, gripping handfuls of sheets and blankets alike.

I can feel myself close to climax when I sit up and stand him up in front of me. I'm not sure exactly how to start what he did to me to him, but I take my best guess and get started. Based off his soft moans and the way he grabbed the back of my hair with both his hands and thrusted in my face, I could tell I was doing a decent job.

He pushed me back on the bed yet again and straddled me, taking all of me inside him. I've had sex with Lydia a couple of times, but it's never felt like this before. It feels oddly right and maybe it's just been a long time since I've been sexual with someone, but it feels tighter than I remember.

Seconds turned into minutes which turned into hours of non-stop fucking. I'll admit that I got curious and even allowed him to enter me. Quickly, I learned that I made too rash a decision when it felt like I had given birth and immediately pushed him away from behind me. Wincing in agonizing pain that seemed to last a minute or so, we laid next to each other and started laughing to ourselves.

As we caught our breath, Benjamin took my face in both his hands and said, "I guess that part isn't for you. How about we continue to do it the way we've been doing it?"

"Agreed!" I said as I started laughing again.

We went at it a few more times before we laid next to each other, cuddling. I noticed his breathing get slower and realized he had fallen asleep the same way Lydia used to- in my arms with our nude bodies against each other.

Oh god. What have I done? Oh Lydia. I'm so sorry.

My sobriety returned hours ago, yet unnatural forces kept me here with Benjamin. I sat up in bed slowly and slid myself out from under the blankets like a snake. I grabbed my clothes from next to the bed and quietly opened the door to Benjamin's bedroom. Stopping in the doorway, I turn to look at his gloriously perfect body one more time and shake my head in disgust.

I close the door quietly and tiptoe down the hall, missing the areas that creak in the hardwood and open my door. I throw my armful of clothes on the floor and shut the door behind me. I can't believe I'd just almost spent the night with a man. Where have my morals gone? I'm damned for all of eternity and for what? A night with a succubus in male form?

I throw myself into bed and shut my eyes, laying there until I finally drift off to sleep.

Tomorrow is a new day.

It's been three weeks since Benjamin and I slept together. The first few days after it happened, I felt so ashamed and embarrassed, but the more I thought about it, the more I wanted to do it again. I've never had an experience like that with Lydia. It was always great when it was with her, but with Benjamin, it feels different.

Most nights as I walk to my bedroom, I notice his door is cracked and he's usually walking around nude, bearing all for the world to see. I usually peek through the crack and watch as he touches his body from his neck down to his waist, all for me to see.

When he notices me, I walk away- too embarrassed to act on any urges I may have. Once I'm in my room, I curse myself for not having the confidence to make my way into his room and ravage him from head to toe. Instead, I masturbate to the memory of three weeks ago, hoping to be caught in the act by him.

Each night, I hope he barges in and handles me like the first time, but each night I find myself growing more and more restless waiting. So, I finally decide that next time I see his door cracked, I'll make it count.

As luck would have it, two nights after hatching up my plan to take him for myself, I notice his door is cracked again. My heart starts to race as I wander closer to the opening, getting excited that my plan is in motion. This time, however, he isn't walking around nude, but clothed. I push the door open and walk in without him noticing.

He turns around and lets out a gasp, "Evan! My god you've just scared the hell out of me. I didn't hear you come in."

"I'm sorry, Benjamin. I didn't mean to startle you. I was just walking past and noticed your door was left open and wanted to check on-"

"You wanted to see if I was naked again, didn't you?" He says with a smirk.

"I- I-" Too stunned to speak after being called out, I ramble on, "I was just curious about why your door was open and why you were pacing back and forth."

Rolling his eyes, "My door is usually open, Evan. I like it that way. I've been in situations where I've had to leave quickly, and I don't want to risk being stuck behind a locked door."

I can't say I'm not disappointed to hear those words. This whole time I'd hoped he was leaving his door cracked for me to bear witness to his chiseled body walking back and forth in the nude each night. Still, I can't explain why he's mostly unclothed and now he is.

"And if you're wondering about the nudity, I usually sleep better when I'm not constricted by undergarments."

Imagining the body that lay just under the clothes he's wearing I feel my heart ready to leap out of my chest. It's taking all of me to not tear the clothes from his body and repeat that first night from three weeks ago.

"I have no clue what you're talking about." I say obliviously.

"Do you think me naive? I've noticed you outside my door glaring at me like a cat staring at a mouse, ready to pounce on its prey. Honestly, I'm flattered. And maybe the nudity was, in part, for your pleasure. But Evan, I'm not playing these games with you anymore."

"What games? I'm not playing a game."

"Don't give me that! The night we shared a few weeks ago was beautiful and it was a lot of fun, but frankly I want something a little more serious. I've played the mouse for too long. I've enjoyed the chase and have wanted nothing more than for you to pounce and claim your prize, but after that night it's like I'm some type of caged animal for you to only gaze upon." He says, sounding a little more hurt than he probably meant to. "I just don't want to be taken advantage of anymore."

Standing there, I had no words. I was embarrassed. Humiliated, even, "Benjamin, I-"

"I think you should go," he says, while ushering me towards the door. Before I know it, I'm standing in the hallway outside his door. "Goodnight, Evan. I'll see you in the morning."

The door all but closes and I shamefully walk across the hall to my bedroom door. I turn before grabbing my doorknob in time to see the light bleeding from the cracked door go dark.

"Goodnight, Benjamin," I whisper. "Sleep tight."

I enter my room and lay in bed. Once the light is out, I lay in the dark, staring at the shadows of the tree outside my window reflecting on the ceiling above my bed. What isn't serious about what we did? Why would he want something that's even more serious?

I drift to sleep thinking of answers to the million and one questions I have for Benjamin. He might have just rejected me, but he'll realize soon what a big mistake he made.

CHAPTER 8

I can't help but to reminisce of my past as I lay in bed, unable to sleep. I haven't slept well since the attack but thinking of the normalcy- or what I thought was normalcy- of life before helps soothe my anxiety.

Once I'm calm, though, I suddenly get angry. I can't help but to think that Sam is still out there somewhere, sleeping soundly, thinking he's gotten away with committing a crime as heinous as the one attempted. No matter how many times I run the scenario through my mind, again and again, I can't seem to figure out his motive. Why waste years building a relationship if the plan was to kill me? Why not just do it and save time? Was it a big game of cat and mouse?

Finally deciding I'd spent enough time staring at the

ceiling, thinking over and over about my attack and the motive behind it, I throw on a heather gray tee shirt and some black sweatpants and make my way downstairs for a nightcap. Passing through the hallway outside of my room, I notice the glow coming from the chandelier in the foyer and hear Julie talking on the phone. I can barely make out what she's saying as I make my way to the balcony, but the words are becoming clearer as I inch closer to the top of the steps.

"Well then when?" She asks with an annoyed tone. "He's been here long enough and I'm not getting anywhere with him. You either come and do it or I'll handle it myself."

I hear a loud slam on the counter as I assume Julie hung up on whomever she was talking to and then forcefully put her phone down. My heart is beating so fast, I barely hear the footsteps walking quickly towards the bottom of the stairs and decide the spot I'm in is no longer a good place to be. I take off back down the hall as quickly as I can towards my room as I hear Julie's footsteps about halfway up the stairs.

Just as I'm about to reach my door, I step on a weak spot on the floor and a loud creaking sound echoes down the hall, causing the footsteps to halt on the staircase. The hesitation and lack of sound is so quiet that it seems like my pulse is echoing louder than the floorboard that gave away my position.

Julie calls out, "Leo? Is that you?"

Realizing that hiding and pretending that I had been in my room the whole time was no longer an option, I take a deep breath and walk back down the hall towards the foyer again.

"Yeah, it's me," My breathing slows while my heart stays racing. "I was thinking I could use a nightcap. Care to join me?"

Seemingly uneasy, she replies, "Of course! You know I can't turn down a late-night drink. I'm going to change into something more comfortable and I'll meet you in the kitchen. Don't get started without me!" She lets out a forced laugh and disappears into the first bedroom on the right.

Confused as to why she entered the bedroom upstairs instead of her own room downstairs, I glance through the door as it shuts abruptly behind her. From the brief view I had just received, the room seems to be used as a giant closet- which makes sense seeing as old houses like these typically didn't have built-in storage for clothing.

Does she not have an armoire in her room like I have in mine? I let the thoughts roll off my shoulders- it's none of my concern. Her house, her weird rules.

I make my way down to the kitchen and stand with my arms shoulder-width apart on the kitchen island. My gut is wrenching and I feel like I could throw up. I keep trying not to take her words out of context but I can't shake the feeling that she was talking about me. Come and do what? She's going to handle *what* herself?

I hear shuffling from the room above the kitchen and remember why I came down here in the first place. I pour myself a bourbon and take a seat at the island across from the sink. With each sip of my drink, I notice my hands are trembling profusely, so I take a couple of deep breaths and close my eyes, trying desperately to focus my thoughts on reason instead of jumping to conclusions.

A couple of minutes later, I hear footsteps approaching the kitchen from the hallway and I turn to face Julie, who is still wearing the same clothes she was going upstairs in.

"Hey! I thought you were going to wait for me!" She says jokingly while heading towards the bar cart, probably to mix herself a gin and tonic as she does most nights.

"I thought you were going to change into something more comfortable," I say curtly.

I notice her shoulders tense and she turns around, "I was going to. Then I remembered it's my house and I'll do as I please."

We stared at each other silently for about twenty seconds before she turned back around and continued mixing a G&T. I took the opportunity to finish my bourbon and stood up from the island counter.

"Having another?" Julie asked with a smile as fake as the hospitality she's providing me apparently.

"No thank you. Wouldn't want to overstep. Seems like I'm doing that enough lately."

Stunned, she replies, "You heard me on the phone just now, huh?"

"I didn't want to, but yes. Why did you let me stay here if I've been such a burden?"

Julie stayed silent and turned back around only after pouring her G&T into the decorative glass she chose from inside the bar cart. She walked over to the kitchen table and sat down, facing the window. I could just barely make eye contact with her reflection as she sipped her cocktail.

"I let you stay here out of the kindness of my heart, Leo. You took advantage of my hospitality the same way I took advantage of having someone to talk to. Do you know how lonely it's been in this big old house? I've been by myself for years and all because I've needed to wait for you to remember. It doesn't work right unless you remember."

"What the fuck are you talking about, Julie? Remember what?" I shout, more confused than angry. "What doesn't work right?"

"That's not how this works, Leo. I can't tell you what you need to remember. You need to find a way to remember. It's like this every single damned time. I'm exhausted. I play the helpful stranger and have to coax you along until your mind finally opens up and you ultimately remember your past."

"You're not making sense! Who were you talking to, Julie? And what are they going to do to me?"

Footsteps approaching from behind startle me and I spin around quickly, just in time to make eye contact with my best friend since high school, "Arie?"

"Hi, Leo." Arie says as she smiles warmly.

"What are you doing here?"

Julie interjects, "She's here to help you remember, Leo. It's been long enough."

"Julie! We agreed to take it slow with him. He's still in a fragile state since the attack."

"Well, he needs to finish this. I'm sick of reliving this nightmare over and over again. And stop calling me Julie. My name is Lydia. Lydia Greene."

CHAPTER 9

The den in Julie's house has been my safe haven these last couple of weeks. The warm glow of the fireplace causing the shadows to waltz around the room used to let my mind wander into my past. The quiet crackle of the extra dry birch piled inside used to let me focus on one idea at a time. Now, however, as the three of us sit equally spaced out on the tastefully decorated sectional opposite the fire, I can't focus. The crackle is drowned out by my own heartbeat and the dancing shadows are ignored by the throbbing headache growing in my frontal lobe.

"You're not making any sense. Lydia? Who's Lydia?" I ask, confused and frustrated.

Julie rolls her eyes and exhales, "I am. My name is Lydia Greene. I've known you for a very long time, Leo."

"So, you've been lying to me this entire time?" I turn to Arie, "And you knew about this?"

Arie opens her mouth to reply, but Julie- I mean, Lydia- cuts her off. "Yes, Arie knew. But in all fairness, we weren't sure you were ready to learn the truth. You've spent the last couple of months recovering and we didn't want you to stress any more than you already are."

I sink my face into my palms and can feel my heartbeat in my fingertips ticking against my forehead.

"Leo, please say something," Arie says, staring at me with sorrowful eyes.

I lift my head and look at Arie, who now is on the verge of tears, "What do you want me to say? I'm confused about all of this. I've been living with someone I thought I knew and my best friend knew the truth this whole time, but chose not to say anything." I say, fighting the urge to want to cry myself. "I just think I need some time to process this."

Nodding her head, Lydia says, "That's understandable. If you need anything, we'll be right here."

"I'm going for a drive," I say, standing up. "Don't wait up."

As I head upstairs to grab my shoes and a light hoodie, I can't help but to think of Sam. All murderous tendencies aside, I really just want to be held closely to his chest and fall asleep listening to his heartbeat and feeling the warmth of his embrace. But like the last few months, he was a lie. Was any of it real? Is everyone lying to me?

I shake my head and rub my eyes. Stop thinking. It's too much lately.

Stopping at my bedroom door with my hand on the doorknob, I take a deep breath. My shoulders feel heavy with the sudden weight of uncertainty. I crack my neck and rub my temples gently to alleviate some of the tension I'm feeling behind my brow before exiting.

I'd been driving around for maybe an hour or so before I could feel my eyelids getting heavy. Seeing signs for a rest stop ahead, I take a couple of deep breaths and decide to stop for a bathroom break and a bottle of water. I look at the clock and I'm not phased in the slightest by the digital "2:12AM" illuminating the top half of my dashboard. Lately, I don't get to sleep until around 3:30 or 4:00, so it's a little unusual to be so tired right now, but not completely out of the question for me.

Pulling into a spot close to the main entrance of the welcome center, I park the car, turn it off, then take the keys out of the ignition. All the while, I'm constantly scanning my surroundings- a couple of semis with parking lights on, indicating a few truckers are more than likely resting before another big haul and a car or two scattered here and there.

Considering it safe, I get out and make my way to the bathroom quickly, hitting the lock button on my key fob an obsessive amount of times, making sure it's locked tight.

Walking through the automatic doors, I take note of the vending machines on my left and head towards the restrooms on my right. Walking into the men's room, I'm engulfed by an awful combination of the smell of piss and shit and fight the urge to vomit. I decide it's best to breathe through my mouth and walk to a urinal at the end of the row.

I arrive at the furthest one and unbutton my pants. Right as I'm about to let the golden river flow, I hear footsteps coming into the bathroom and it's like my urethra tightens, acting as a dam preventing anything from escaping. I decide not to look at my pissing companion- mostly for my own dignity, but a little for "bro code"- and take a couple of short breaths before the stream begins again.

I'm so focused on my breathing that I don't notice my companion standing at the urinal next to me. Of all fifteen urinals, the one next to me seemed the nicest, I guess. Then I feel his stare. Out of my peripheral, I can make out his face looking towards me. I slowly turn my head and make eye contact with a man about ten or so years older than me. He was certainly attractive, but in a normal, nonsexual kind of way.

He smirks, "What's up, dude?" His eyes wandering down my body, stopping where my hands are blocking the view of my dick.

"Just trying to do my business." I say, ignoring his amateur attempt at cruising.

"Aw come on! You're not gonna make me beg for it, are you?" He turns toward me, exposing his fully erect penis, reaching towards mine.

"Don't touch me, dude!" I say, zipping up my jeans as I hurry towards the sink to wash my hands.

Great! It seems like all of the soap dispensers are empty.

Making his way towards me, the stranger says, "Bro, just let me touch it! I promise I won't tell your girlfriend."

Every single fucking one. Fantastic. No soap in this whole bathroom.

"I'll be quick, don't worry. I clean up my messes too. No evidence left behind- I swear!" He keeps trying. Gotta admire his persistence.

Fuck it! I'll use the hand sanitizer in my car. I turn around and move towards the exit. Before I get more than a few steps away, I feel a hand grab my shoulder and spin me around. The man then shoves me up against the wall and grabs at my crotch, trying to unbutton and unzip my jeans.

Pushing him away, I sprint towards the welcome center exit and arrive at my car. I'm looking in the direction I had just ran from and don't see the creep anywhere. Before I have a chance to calm myself down, my heart sinks further and I have the urge to vomit yet again.

Shit. Shit! I can't find my keys.

After having spent about ten minutes searching the area around my car and in the flowerbeds leading up to the main entrance of the welcome center, I manage to muster up the courage to walk back into the bathroom to find my keys. I know for sure that creep is still in there, most likely with dick still in hand.

It's fine. In and out. Get the keys and leave.

As the automatic doors slide open, my heart starts beating faster with each step towards the men's room. I walk in and to my surprise, he's nowhere to be seen. Luckily, I see my keys on the floor under the sink counter and bend down to reach for them. As I'm hunched over, I hear a stall door fling open and steps approaching me fast.

"Come back for more, baby?" The man says as he runs at me, now bearing all.

I dodge him at the last second and he slams into the waist-height counter hard. He's too quick because before I know it, he's already turned in my direction and coming after me yet again.

"Get away from me! Help!" I shout out hoping someone- anyone- could hear me and come to my rescue.

Just as I'm running towards the exit, the man grabs my hood and pulls me down, causing me to fall hard on my back, knocking the air from my lungs. Taking not of my newfound weakness, the man straddles my chest, smacking my face with his hard dick, trying to shove it in my mouth. His knees are holding my arms down and his weight isn't allowing for much room to resist.

Somehow though, I manage to bring both my legs up and wrap them around his neck, MMA-style and pull him back towards the ground. I must have done it hard because when his head hit the tile floor, the sound reverberated throughout the bathroom with a sickening crack.

Using my now-free arms, I manage to pull myself out from under the weight of the man and I pick myself up off the floor. The man isn't moving, so my guess is he's unconscious. I start to panic as the thought of me accidentally killing him sets in.

What will happen to me? Will anyone believe that he tried attacking me? What will they think of this random, naked man lying on the floor? It was self defense. That's all. He attacked me and I defended myself by any means necessary.

Just as the thoughts start rolling in my head of creating solid alibis, I notice his chest is moving up and down slowly. He's alive, but he doesn't look like he's doing good-definitely has a concussion at the very least. Going against my better judgement to leave his naked ass in that dirty bathroom, I decide the right thing to do is call 9-1-1. Even if he doesn't deserve the help, I can't just leave someone like this.

I pull out my phone and start to dial when I hear the man start to move. My attention is drawn away from the small screen and towards the man who has started to sit up, grabbing the back of his head where he had just cracked the small tile underneath of him. He brings his hand back in front of his face and notices minuscule traces of blood on his fingers.

"What did you just do, you son-of-a-bitch? You tried to kill me?" He says, getting noticeably angrier and angrier with each question. "Do you have a fucking death wish, boy?"

"I told you to stay away, but you-"

"Lucky for you, I love a good fight." Standing now, he's blocking my path out of the men's room. "You made me bleed. Now I'm gonna make you wish you were dead."

He starts to run at me, and I freeze. I don't know what else to do besides stand there and take whatever he's about to give me.

Just as quick as he starts towards me, he steps in a puddle of someone's urine and his feet slide out from under him, causing him to go down fast. On his way down this time, however, the sink counter catches the side of his head hard and I hear a louder crack than the one before.

When I hear his dead weight hit the tile, I wait a little longer, holding my breath. My hands start to tremble as I no longer see his chest moving up and down. Chills run down my spine as I make eye contact with his lifeless body. Somehow, I also feel relieved- that I'm no longer in danger and the fight is over.

Realizing I had never gotten the chance to pick up my keys before he appeared the second time, I looked past his balding head and saw them still up against the wall underneath the sink counter. It's interesting to think of something sitting still while the world around it is going to hell. At the same time, it's oddly comforting.

I wipe the tears from my face and I can feel my expression harden. I step over the slop of a man that tried to rape, then kill me and reach down to grab my keys for the second time tonight. I stand up, face the mirror, and wash my hands in the sink above his head. Grabbing a few paper towels from the dispenser on the wall next to the mirror, I dry my hands thoroughly and ball up the now-saturated towels in my hands.

I take one last look at the man lying before me and toss the waste onto his lifeless body.

"Fuck you. Fuck. You."

On my way out of the bathroom, I notice the vending

machines and realize I still hadn't gotten the bottle of water I so desperately needed just twenty minutes ago. I reach into my pocket and pull out a crumpled dollar bill. The satisfying sound of the machine eating the currency from the palm of my hand comforts me as I make my selection.

When the bottle drops below, I reach down to grab my prize from the cubby and to my surprise, find another bottle of water just like mine. Someone forgot to claim theirs, but I can't help but to think this was the universe's way of apologizing for my night. I sink to my knees and can't hold back the tears anymore.

How pathetic it must look to the security guards watching this tape tomorrow to see a man in his twenties crying over a bottle of water. In that moment, I sit up straight, wiping the tears from my cheeks and begin scanning the room I'm in for any cameras.

Thank God. None.

I pick myself up off the floor, grabbing both bottles of water and make my way to my car quickly. Once inside, I strap myself in, turn the key in the ignition, and leave that horrible welcome center in my rearview. I barely notice the lack of music on the hour-long drive on the way home because my thoughts are so loud they'd have drowned them out anyway.

I pull into the driveway slowly, turning the car off as I park. Instead of going inside, I tilt my seat back as far as it will go and shut my eyes. All of my energy had been drained back at the welcome center and I couldn't possibly find any good reason to go inside the house of betrayal tonight.

My thoughts seem to subside at the same time I drift to sleep.

CHAPTER 10

The morning after Benjamin called off our arrangement, I woke up before the sunrise and decided to go for a walk. It's been a long time since I've watched the sun rise over the gardens of my family home- even longer since I've had a reason to. It's always been a nice way of distracting myself from everyday life. The way the first rays of the morning light reflect on the dew drops creates almost miniature magnifying glasses reflecting light across the yard. One could confuse the lights with diamonds resting on the perfectly manicured hedges and flowers strewn about the yard.

This morning feels even more deserved, however, as I play with the ideas of how I want my life to continue. I have some very important choices to make and each one of them will dictate a certain aspect of my life. I take a seat in a small bistro set surrounded by roses- a wonderful sight to behold. It's a struggle to contain my thoughts, but I try to focus on one idea at a time.

Do I continue the path set forward by my parents and marry a woman I have no relationship with just for the sake of bearing children? Or do I follow my heart and confess my love for Benjamin, completely uprooting any idea of continuing the family legacy through traditional means?

"Good morning, darling." My mother says as she approaches me.

"Good morning, Mother. I didn't hear you coming." I say as I straighten my posture in my chair. "Care for some tea?"

"I would love a cup. Did Benjamin make this? I didn't realize he was awake." She looks around the yard and then back at the house inquisitively.

"No, Benjamin is more than likely still asleep. I made it myself when I came downstairs. I wasn't sleeping well enough so I thought it best to get an early start to my day."

"Oh thank God! The tea is awful when Benjamin makes it!" She laughs whole-heartedly. "I'd be better off with a spoonful of dirt and lukewarm water."

My mother's laugh is contagious- always has been. Even with my heart sunken in my chest and my consciousness on the verge of a meltdown, I still manage to laugh with her. Moments like these are often overlooked and taken for granted. Depending on my choice, these moments may just turn to memories.

The smile on my face slowly fades as the reality of my situation comes more to light. My hands start to tremble and I feel a bead of sweat run down the nape of my neck.

"Mother, there's something I wish to discuss with you, if I may," I say, almost swallowing my tongue.

"Of course, dear. What is it?" She sips her tea and turns her head to me, the morning light shining on her ocean-blue eyes, causing them to glow slightly.

Heart pounding in my chest, pulse throbbing in my neck, I turn my head to her, "I'm in love."

"You're in love?" She asks with excitement. "With whom? Was she at the party? I didn't think any of the young ladies there caught your eye."

"Mother, I-"

"Your father will be so happy to hear of this! Oh Evan! This is amazing news, indeed."

"No, Mother, I-"

"And the wedding! I can finally start planning the wedding. How do you feel about apricot? The color would only do your skin tone justice. And-"

"Mother, I'm in love with Benjamin!" I interject.

Mother quiets herself and looks at me with an expression I'd never seen from her before. She picks up her teacup and takes another sip, turning to face the garden.

"Please say something," I beg, tears welling in my eyes. I'd never been this vulnerable with her before and now, after telling her my biggest secret, I can see why I'd never allowed myself the opportunity. "Please."

We sat in silence for a full six minutes before she shifted in her seat and refilled her tea. The orange glow of the morning light is fading to a more subtle yellow color.

"I can't say I'm surprised," She says, startling me when she broke her silence.

"You're not surprised?" I say, sniffling and wiping the tears from my eyes. "How do you mean?"

"Evan, I'm your mother. I can tell when something is off with you. And frankly, darling, you've been staring at Benjamin since he arrived. The boy has practically had to follow you around the house to clean up a river of your saliva."

"Was I that obvious?" I ask worriedly, "Does Father know?"

"I don't think your father would ever notice something happening right in front of his face." She waves her hands and lets out a howl of a laugh, causing me to jump.

"What do you think he'll say when I tell him?"

"Oh, you won't. Not yet anyway. We need to prepare him for this. Until I can come up with a few different ideas on how to go about this, please keep this to yourself. Go about your business as usual. And I don't know- try to pretend like you're interested in the female suitors he invites for you. If anything- just to keep up the charade."

Nodding my head, I reply, "Of course. Thank you, Mother. Thank you for understanding."

"Oh, I definitely do not understand it, but you're my son, Evan. And if you're choosing to be happy, then I cannot stand in the way of that happiness. If you say you're ready for it, then I support any decision you choose to make. You're still my biggest love."

The tears start falling again as I hug my mother for what feels like an eternity.

"I love you, Mother."

"I love you, too, Evan. Always have and always will."

CHAPTER 11

It's been two days since the attack at the welcome center. I haven't even told the girls yet. Even though the event is one of major trauma, my sleep is unaltered, surprisingly. My dreams are peaceful, which is more than I can say for my waking thoughts. While I'm awake, I picture over and over again that man slipping and hitting his head. It's as if it's on a loop playing repeatedly in my mind.

Did he have a family? Or at least someone who would miss him if he died?

I decide I've had enough self-torture and venture downstairs to grab some breakfast. It's concerning how with everything I've been through this past year that I still have an appetite- especially after two nights ago. I hear

Lydia and Arie talking about that night and stop in my tracks in the hallway outside the kitchen.

"Did you see on the news? Some guy was found dead at the welcome center. Police are saying blunt force trauma was the thing that did him in. Weirdest part is he was found completely naked." Lydia says as she pours a fresh cup of coffee and passes it to Arie.

"I heard from a girl at work! It's kind of nerve-racking if you think about it. Someone gets killed so close to home and they hardly have any theories as to who did it," Arie says while blowing on her piping hot cup of Joe. "Do you think it was-"

"No. What reason would he have had to kill some innocent man?" Lydia replies. "This was someone else. It had to be."

"Wasn't Leo driving around that night?"

"Don't even think it! There's no way he would've done something like that."

Arie shrugs her shoulders and takes another sip of her coffee. "I mean, should we ask him? Just to be sure?"

They barely notice me standing in the hallway before I continue towards them. "Good morning, ladies." I say, nonchalantly.

"Morning, Leo!" Lydia says, more excitedly than she normally would- probably trying to play off the fact that they were just talking about me. "How'd you sleep?"

"I slept pretty great actually! And no- I didn't kill anybody," I say as I open the cupboard to grab a mug.

Both of them fall silent as I turn around with the coffee carafe in my hand.

"We didn't think-" Arie starts.

"He killed himself. It was a complete accident." I say, not making eye contact with either of them. You could cut the tension in the room with a hot knife. "And honestly guys- I'm kind of freaking out about it."

"Leo, what happened?" Lydia's expression becomes empathetic as she puts a hand on my shoulder. "We're here for you. You can tell us anything."

Nodding her head, Arie continues, "Yeah. If something is going on, let us help."

Tears filling my eyes, I explain to them the story of what happened two nights ago when I had my encounter with the dead guy from the TV. By the time I had explained everything, the three of us were sobbing together.

Standing up straight and wiping away her tears, Lydia took out a wineglass and twisted open a fresh bottle of merlot.

Also wiping her tears, Arie asks, "Isn't it a little early for wine?" She gestures towards the stove clock that reads: "9:43AM."

"Well it's not every day that your friend drops a bomb on you like this. Feels like a stay at home and get drunk kind of day." She pours a large glass and then drinks a long gulp out of the bottle directly.

Arie and I laugh loudly and grab our own glasses.

"The merlot is mine- but feel free to help yourselves to whatever other booze we have." She chuckles but gives us a look that lets us know she's serious.

Around two in the afternoon, we had already gone through four bottles of wine, a bottle of peach schnapps and we were working on a bottle of cheap Prosecco. Arie had fallen asleep drunk and was laying in between Lydia and I on the couch. We were watching *The Notebook* and cheering with a clink of our glasses every time Ryan Gosling took off his shirt.

I looked over at Lydia, "Thank you for this, Lydia. Thank you for everything really. I appreciate everything you've done for me and everything you're still doing."

"You're very welcome, Evan. Anything I can do to help."

My mind flashes back to a warm day sitting in a garden with a woman a little older than Lydia is now.

"Evan?" I say, taken back by the déjà vu I just experienced. "Who's Evan?"

"Did I say Evan?" She says, shocked by her mistake.

"You did. And when you called me Evan, I saw a woman sitting in a garden that looked similar to your backyard."

"Then that's it! That's how we fix your memory!" She exclaims.

"Fix my memory? To help me remember what you and Arie want me to remember so badly?"

"Exactly!" She replies quickly.

"What do we have to do?" I ask, curiously.

"Leo," she starts, looking at me seriously, "We need to find your mother."

"My mother?" I ask- confused about why we would need to get in touch with that awful woman. "How could she possibly help us?"

"Not your current mother- your old mother." Lydia says.

"Oh, this again? The mom from my past life right?" I roll my eyes.

I don't know why, but Lydia and Arie both keep trying to make me remember some science fiction bullshit about a past life. It's really frustrating me lately. It's like they're both living in this fantasy world.

"Roll your eyes all you want, Leo. That doesn't change the fact that it's real. You may not remember what we need you to, but that doesn't make it anything less than what it is. Your old mother has to have information. If Arie and I remember, then chances are she does too."

Crossing my arms, I look at her with puzzling eyes. "And how do you propose we get ahold of this 'Old-Mother?'" I say, unfolding my arms only to make air quotations.

"Well that part is easy. We have to get ahold of your brother first."

"Alex? You're not telling me he's been in on this, too?" I drop my arms and sit up straight. "You said so yourself- he hasn't answered anytime you called and I haven't heard from him since before Sam put me in the hospital."

"So that was a lie. Arie and I have already been in contact with Alex. He's well aware of the plan to get you to remember. He's wanted to come check in on you, but we weren't sure if you were ready yet. We're so close to getting you to remember, I can feel it. Now is as good a time as any."

"So then who was Alex in my past? My father? A fish?" I can't help but be sarcastic when I'm uncomfortable. It just helps me cope, I guess.

"No. Alex was my adopted brother and his name was Henry. It just so happens that he's now yours. I know it's all confusing, Leo. But you have to trust us." Lydia looks at me with pleading eyes.

Strangely enough- I do trust Lydia and Arie. Even though what they're saying is absolutely unbelievable, I trust they have the best intentions.

Sighing, I say, "I do trust you. It's just a lot all at once."

Taking a deep breath, I continue, "What do you need me to do?"

Lydia smiles as she jumps up from the couch, waking Arie at the same time. Arie yawns and stretches out her arms, "What's going on?" She asks with tired eyes.

"What's going on is we're reaching out to Alex." I say as Arie's eyes widen. She, too, jumps up from the couch and looks at Lydia.

"Is he ready?" She asks.

Lydia turns around after grabbing her phone off the kitchen island. "He's as ready as he'll ever be, Arie. Get yourself ready, both of you. I'm gonna call Alex and we'll meet him in town."

Arie looks at me while smiling apologetically and then heads upstairs to the spare room next to mine. I follow suit and head upstairs to change and brush my teeth. The buzz I had before is now long gone and I can see clearly now how much work is to be done.

When I'm in my room, I pick out something quick- a Dodgers jersey and a pair of faded, ripped jeans with my white, slip-on Vans. Looking for a baseball cap, I settle for a white Under Armour one. Before I head back downstairs, I stop in front of the mirror and admire myself.

For the first time in forever, I like what I see. The time I spent in the hospital and my lack of appetite recently have thinned me out to the point that I look lean and vascular.

I stand there, twisting this way and that and can't help but to smile. I've come a long way and been through too much to keep hating myself.

Lydia calls from downstairs and it breaks my daydream. "Guys, let's go! Alex is gonna meet us there. Who's good to drive?"

"I am!" I call out. I check myself out one last time before I head downstairs. "Give me the keys!"

"Absolutely fucking not," Lydia says. "You're way too gone to get behind the wheel right now."

"I'm good- really! I don't feel it anymore." I

"Why don't we call a Lyft?" Arie asks. "It'd be better than *almost* making it there."

"Good idea," Lydia replies.

When the three of us arrive in town, we step out of the ride-share and onto the sidewalk. We had decided to meet at the little cafe in town that sits adjacent to the diner where Sam and I had our first date. As I'm scoping out the area, making sure there's no sign of that devil, I hear a car alarm beep.

"There he is! Man of the hour!" I hear my brother's all-too-familiar voice and turn around to face him. "How have you been, bro?"

"Alex!" I exclaim as I go in for a hug. "I've been good, man. How have you been?"

"Ah, you know how it is. Working all day and then barely sleeping all night," he says with a shrug.

"So the usual?"

We both laugh and he puts his hand on my shoulder. "Seriously though, bro. Are you okay? I wanted to reach out, but-"

"I know- it just wasn't a good time. But you're here now, so that's all that matters." I look at my brother with forgiving eyes and he nods.

"Let's get a coffee, shall we? The tab is on me."

Once inside, the four of us place our coffee orders and sit at a table close to the door. As we're sitting, I can't shake the feeling that I'm being watched. I start scanning my surroundings, looking for any sign of someone watching me. I only see the occasional car pass by or the random lone jogger run past the window outside, but no one steadily watching me.

"Leo- are you okay?" Arie catches me off guard. "You drifted off just now."

"Sorry, I was just thinking." I lied because I don't want anymore sympathy. They're already giving me too much. "What were you guys saying?"

Lydia starts, "Well, Alex said he's pretty sure he knows where your mom has been all these years. But- and it's a big but- he's not sure she remembers either. So that's a bit of a problem for us."

"Well if she doesn't remember then what's the point of reaching out to her?" I say. "After all, I feel like she'll be just as confused as I am.

Alex adjusts in his chair, "That's the other reason I'm here. I need to help you remember too. It's super important that you remember the past. Did you ladies tell him why?" He looks at Lydia and Arie in an expecting way.

The girls look at each other and shake their heads.

"Great," he turns back to me. "Well you need to know how to stop whatever this cycle is. You may not remember, but the rest of us do. This isn't the first time that our souls have come in contact with each other. Haven't you ever wondered why you feel like some things are familiar?"

"I mean yeah, but I just thought it was déjà vu. I didn't think anything of it beyond that."

"That's a lie." Lydia says assertively. "When I called you Evan earlier, you had a *That's So Raven* moment and spaced out. You told me you had a vision of you and your mom in the garden at the house."

Alex continues, "Okay so that's definitely progress! You're remembering small things, but what we really need is for you to remember everything."

"Why is it so important for me to remember everything? What aren't you telling me?" Now it's harder to hide that

I'm getting pissed off. I continue, "It's like you guys have an inside joke that you won't let me in on. It's driving me crazy. Why and *what* do I need to remember exactly?"

The three of them share glances with each other and Alex turns to me. "Because if you remember your past, it could help you stop Sam."

"Stop Sam? Stop him from what, exactly?"

"You could stop Sam from killing you again, Leo."

"Alex, you sound insane. What are you even talking about?" My voice cracks with a bit of nervousness and anger. "Killing me- again?"

He sips his coffee and Lydia starts, "In each life the two of you share, Sam manages to kill you. It's usually after he gets to know you and you both establish a relationship. Each time, Arie and I are close to stopping him, but the two of you are drawn to each other. We can never stop you from falling for him and eventually he kills you. The last time, we didn't even realize it was him until it was too late. This time, I was following you in the park that day. Something in my gut told me to stay close, but when I ran into a couple of friends, I got distracted. Luckily- I got to you before he could finish what he set out to do."

I sat back in my chair, trying to grasp what Lydia just told me. "We're drawn to each other? If he kills me in every life, then what's different this time? And why does he waste his time over and over again with getting to know me if the end result is the same?"

"That's what we're trying to figure out." Arie answers. "It's like it's a game for him. He wants to live this perfect life, but eventually something inside him snaps and it's game over for you."

"What about the rest of you? How do you fit in to all this?" I say, waiting for a valid answer.

Alex shrugs his shoulders, "Honestly- we don't know. We usually get to live out the rest of our lives how we see fit, but then it happens all over again. That's why we think it has to do with you stopping him before he kills you. It's only a matter of time before he realizes that you're still alive- if he hasn't already figured that part out. It may seem selfish what I'm about to say, but please listen with an open mind."

I nod as he continues, "We need you to remember so this is the last time. We're tired. Sure, it's a different life with different people and different opportunities. But with all of that comes new problems, new enemies, and new memories we have to live with over and over again. If our theory is correct and you can somehow figure out a way to stop him before he kills you, it may break the cycle we all share. That's why we're so obsessed with you remembering. Plus- we don't want you to die again, of course."

I run over everything they all just said again and again in my head. I could get up and walk out, but if what they're saying is true, then it is absolutely up to me to stop this. I could laugh in their faces and ask where the cameras are. And I could end up waking up from an ongoing nightmare. But instead, I sip my coffee and look out the window.

"Okay," I say. "Let's get my memories back."

CHAPTER 12

My mother has stayed true to her word. She has not yet told my father I'm in love with a man. I think she's trying to accept it herself first, but either way, it has been more than a week and the anticipation of my parents' conversation is killing me.

Benjamin still has not spoken with me, either. The tension is heavy when we cross paths each day, but nothing more than a "good morning" or "goodnight" is said between the both of us. This night, however, I'm tired of waiting for him to acknowledge me. After dinner, I will make the first advance and see how he reacts. He wants a relationship that's serious, but he won't take the time to see the progress I'm making for him.

Silence befalls the dining table while the dinner is being served. My mother keeps looking from me to Benjamin and then back at me with a smile on her face. My face burns with embarrassment, but Benjamin hardly seems to notice as he makes the plates for the three of us.

"Will you be needing anything else Mr. and Mrs. Williams?" He asks as he sets the extra food in the center of the table.

"No, Benjamin, that will be all for now, thank you." My father says, smiling at him unaware that the man before him holds my heart in between his tightly grasped hands.

"Thank you, sir. If you don't mind, I will retire to my chambers until you are finished dinner. I'm not feeling all too well."

"Oh heavens," my mother says. "Please take care, Benjamin. Get some rest- I'll tidy this up when we're finished."

"Thank you, ma'am. Have a good night, Mr. and Mrs. Williams." He looks at me for the first time all night, "Goodnight, Evan."

"Goodnight!" I say, a little too expressively. "Be well, Benjamin."

He nods his head and turns away, heading up the stairs. My heart starts pounding in my chest as he stops a few steps up and turns towards me with that look he used to give when we first started seeing each other. I cough, nearly choking on a piece of potato and he smirks, continuing up the steps. Wiping my mouth, I continue eating and reassure my parents that I'm alright.

After finishing my food in record time, I stand up from my place at the table, "May I also be excused? I think I may sleep early. I'd like to get an early start tomorrow."

"Absolutely, Son." My father says, looking at me questioningly. "What changed? Is my son finally tired of wasting the morning away sleeping in?" He chuckles and my mother laughs along with him.

"Precisely, Father. I'm tired of wasting my life away. I'm ready to grab my life with both hands and embrace all that it is."

Wiping the corner of his mouth, my father looks at me with approval, "Very well. Goodnight, Son."

"Goodnight, Darling," my mother says, smiling wide.

"Goodnight, Mother- Father." I start towards the stairs a little too excitedly and decide to slow my pace as to not seem too eager to get upstairs with another boy.

I walk upstairs and start walking down the hall slowly, noticing Benjamin's door is cracked. I get close and slowly open it, ready to see what's waiting for me. Only- when I push the door open, I see no one. Benjamin must be in the bathroom, then. I'll wait for him in my room.

I pull the door back to its starting position and cross the hall. Opening my door, I go inside quietly, closing it gently. Before the door latches, I feel hands place themselves over my eyes in the darkness.

"What took you so long?" Benjamin whispers in my ear, his warm breath causing the hairs on my neck to stand at attention.

"I wasn't sure you were even interested in me

anymore," I whisper back, turning around to see his silhouette in the moonlight of the night through my window behind him. I can tell he isn't wearing an ounce of clothing. I continue, "But I can see now that I was mistaken."

"You certainly were, Mr. Williams." He says, causing the fire inside me to burn even hotter. I lurch forward and wrap my arms around his waist, pulling his naked body against mine. I can feel his penis, hard as a rock against my thigh and I kiss his neck deeply, running my hand down his backside and in between his glutes slowly. He lets out a slight moan as I provide pressure while I'm visiting that spot I've visited only a handful of times before.

He pushes me away while dropping to his knees. I can feel him unbuttoning my trousers and pulling them to my ankles. The warmth of his mouth around my groin causes me to close my eyes hard as I run my fingers through his dark locks. I grab the back of his head, forcing him further onto it and hold him there until he chokes quietly. I pull him back by a handful of hair I'd managed to grab onto and bend down to kiss him passionately.

The night is warm and the bedroom is warmer than usual. I can feel the sweat start running down my lower back as I stand him up and shove him against the wall, backside facing me. I give little warning as I thrust my member inside his tight, rear end. He gives almost no protest as I grab onto his hips and continue going in and out.

The only sounds coming from the both of us are

our breath and some very intimate moans. As I edge closer and closer, I remove myself from inside him and lay on my stomach on the bed.

"Your turn," I say, lifting my hips in the air and arching my back as much as I possibly can.

"Are you sure?" He asks as he makes his way towards me in the dark.

"Now- before I change my mind." I lay face down on my pillows as I hear him spit into his hand. Moments later, I feel him enter me. The pain hits me immediately, but I don't move away. It only lasts a couple of seconds before the pleasure arrives and I find myself enjoying having him inside of me.

It doesn't take much before I feel him breathing harder and harder on the back of my neck and then I feel his body having small convulsions as he sinks deeper into my backside. He pulls his member out of me and lays on his back next to where I'm still lying face down.

"That was-" He starts.

"Amazing?" I finish his sentence for him. "I think we found another way to make our arrangement a little more interesting."

It's dark, but I can still make out a smile stretching across his face. "I think you're right."

He turns onto his side, facing me directly and I feel his fingers lightly trace the hilly landscape of my back muscles all the way down to my backside where he squeezes one of my cheeks.

"Evan, I want to apologize."

"Benjamin-"

"No, please let me. This lifestyle isn't something I would wish on anyone. It comes with a history of heartbreak and I hate myself for forcing it upon you."

"I love you."

"And when you love some-" He pauses. "You what?"

"I love you more than anyone I've ever come to know. Ever since you came to this house, I've been drawn to you and I can't explain why. All I know is over these last few months I've grown to love you. Is it madness? Yes. But are you worth it? Yes. I want nothing more than to find a way to be with you. No matter what it takes."

Benjamin grabs my face in his hands and pulls himself closer. His soft, full lips engulf mine and we kiss deeply for a few minutes.

"I love you, too, Evan." He says as he reaches underneath of me, grabbing my member in his hand. I can see him becoming erect again and this time he switches sides and faces his backside in my direction.

"Your turn," He says as I slide inside of him.

The next morning, I'm awakened by a shriek and I immediately leap out of bed, confused as to where Benjamin has run off too. I throw on a robe and fling my door open, yelling down the hall, "Mother! What is it?"

"Evan! It's your father! He isn't breathing!" She yells back, panic in her voice.

I run down the hall and throw my parents'

bedroom door open. Sobbing, my mother is kneeling at my father's side of the bed, shaking him- trying to wake him up. I'm frozen in place as I notice his eyes are open and his face is a purple-blue color.

"Mother, stop."

"He won't wake up, Evan! No matter how hard I try, he just won't wake up." My mother cries harder now.

"Mother- I said stop!" I shout at her, alarming even myself as she lets go of my father and crawls backwards up against the wall, letting her head fall to her knees.

I inch closer and closer to my father's body and can see his tongue sticking out of his mouth ever so slightly. The evidence is clear- my father was suffocated as he tried to sleep.

"Did you come with Father to bed last night?" I say, as calmly as I can to my mother.

"N- no." She sniffles in between syllables. "He came to bed before me. I fell asleep on the parlor couch. I only just came up to check on him right now and found him like this-" She reaches out towards him again, so I intercept her hands and hug her tightly.

It isn't making sense. If he came upstairs and my mother fell asleep downstairs, then the only way he could have been suffocated is- I shudder and feel the goosebumps run across my arms- Benjamin.

"Mother- where's Benjamin? Have you seen him this morning?"

She shakes her head as she sinks into my chest. "I haven't seen Benjamin since last night after he served us supper."

I stand up, "I'll be right back. I need to find Benjamin."

Closing the bedroom door behind me, I decide to check his chambers first. When I get to his door, I can still see it cracked open from how I left it the night before. Deciding it's worth another look anyway, I throw the door open causing it to crash into the wall behind it, leaving a small indent where the doorknob is.

"Benjamin!" I yell, though he's nowhere to be seen.

I check my bedroom again, just to make sure he didn't slip past my parents' bedroom door when I wasn't looking. When I open my door, I see no one. I'd wished to see him still twisted in the bedsheets from the night before, but to my disappointment, they're empty.

I check the other rooms upstairs and again, I see no one. I hear the clang of glass hitting glass downstairs and take off towards the staircase. Barely touching each step on the way down, I swing myself around the banister and start down the hallway to the kitchen. As I enter, his back is facing towards me.

"Benjamin." I say. He doesn't even flinch. I expected him to at least jolt a bit. "What have you done?"

He turns around, smiling, giving me chills down my spine. "What have I done? I've freed you, Evan. Now we can be together."

"Oh God, Benjamin." I say, shocked at the realization that my love killed my father. "Did you- No. You didn't have to kill him!"

"Evan, I had to do this for us. Your father was

never going to let you be with a man. I heard your mother bringing up the idea to him in the parlor last night and he was full of so much hate. I couldn't bear to let him hurt you. Or us!"

"So you killed him? In cold blood? He would have come around! What have you done!"

"I did what I had to do. Does that make me a monster?"

"Yes! It certainly does!" I shout, increasingly more aware of the pitch of my voice. I take a deep breath and try to steady myself against the counter. "I want you gone. Now."

"Evan, don't be rash. I did this for-"

"Out. Now."

Benjamin steps back, emotionless. "Fine. Then let me gather my things and I'll be on my way." I nod and he leaves the kitchen.

I'll have to take mother and get away from here. That much is clear. I'm sure she won't want to stay in this house anymore- I know I don't. Benjamin has ruined the house that holds all memories of my life.

I take a deep breath and I make my way to the parlor to pour myself a large glass of scotch. Sitting back on the couch, I lean my head back and rub my eyes. My head is pounding behind my brow as I hear a shriek come from upstairs.

"Mother!"

I stand quickly, dropping the crystal glass on the floor, causing scotch to flow in every direction. Running upstairs, I skip every other step along the way, getting to the top in record timing. I notice the door is already wide open and peer inside as I round the corner. Standing with his back facing me is Benjamin- his shoulders are moving heavily because of his breathing.

The floor beneath me creaks slightly and I see his back tighten. He turns towards me and when he finally faces me, he smiles. "Evan- glad you could join us." In his hand, a knife. At his feet, my mother's lifeless body.

Benjamin starts walking towards me slowly, "Evan, don't you see? There's no one holding us back now. We can finally be together with no obstacles. I was content with just getting your father out of the picture, but look what you made me do. Your mother didn't have to die, but you forced my hand."

"Benjamin, put the knife down." I say as I start backing up into the hallway. "Let's talk about this."

"What's there to talk about? I gave us a way to be together forever. All you have to do it agree to be mine."

"You're mad if you think I'll ever be yours now."

Standing in place, he remains silent for a few seconds before he replies, "You just had to break my heart, didn't you?"

Backing myself up against the wall, I decide to try to run for it. I only get to turn my body before Benjamin sticks his foot out, tripping me. I fall hard on the landing at the top of the staircase and barely have time to flip over before Benjamin leaps on top of me. Straddling my waist, he raises the knife with both of his hands above his head and starts to bring it towards my chest quickly.

I grab his arms and manage to keep the knife a small distance from my skin.

"Why are you doing this?" I say through gritting teeth, trying to muster whatever strength I have to keep the knife from entering my chest cavity.

"Because you broke my heart, Evan. I was happy at first and now it's just pain." He readjusts himself, leaning forward some to put more of his weight on top of the knife, bringing it to my skin.

The point of the knife breaks the surface of my chest and I feel the cold steel slice layer upon layer until I realize I can move my lower half a little more now that Benjamin isn't sitting on it as much. I manage to lift my thighs swiftly, launching him through the banister at the top of the foyer. He cries out in fear as I send him crashing down onto the table in the center of the room, obliterating it in the process.

I wince as I sit up, drained of all the energy I didn't know I had. While the knife had indeed entered my chest, it wasn't life threatening. I few bandages will do, I think. Standing up, I look over what used to be the intact railing and see Benjamin's eyes looking up at me, unmoving.

Did I just kill him? I make my way slowly down the staircase, holding onto the railing along the journey. Once at the bottom, I approach my former lover's body, inspecting the area for the knife he only just had moments ago. Panic sets in as I lose hope of ever finding it.

I decide it's best to leave the room and go to the kitchen to grab another knife for protection. Grabbing the first one I see, a steak knife from dinner the night before, I start towards the foyer again. As I enter the hallway, a chill flows down my spine as I can no longer see Benjamin's body. The front door is open as if he had run out while I was in the kitchen.

I lightly step towards the front door, knife pointed out in front of me. With each step closer, I can feel the outside breeze entering the room around me. It smells sweet, like the honeysuckle growing along the fence at the front of the property. The breeze is warm, too-reminiscent of a beautiful spring day.

I'm standing on the front stoop now, aware that Benjamin isn't outside, but instead wanted to distract me from the fact that he was behind me. The creak of the floor gives away his position and yet- I don't turn around. If these are in fact my last moments, I want to remember the glistening diamonds strewn about the manicured lawn. I want to remember the smell of the sweet honeysuckle flower floating across the warm breeze on its way to me, my hair swaying slightly in the current-like flow.

It isn't long before the peace I'm feeling is met with pain. The knife slides into my back more slowly than I'd imagined it would. It slides out, then back in again. I let out a scream, but it isn't enough reason for him to stop. I fall to my side on the threshold of my family home, looking up at him, tears in my eyes.

"I loved you, Benjamin." I manage to sputter as the cold sets in.

"I know you did. And I, you, Evan." He replies, emotionless.

I can feel the warmth flow from my back as I lie in the doorway as still as I can. Any type of movement flares the pain ten-fold so I just lay there and accept my fate.

"Tell me something." I say, pain carrying heavily in my voice.

"What's that?"

"Why? Why would you come into my life just to take it away from me?"

His face, still unchanging; his eyes, dead, he says, "Because I was hired to kill you. Your family was collateral. You were my target. It just so happened that I fell in love along the way, making this harder."

Feeling colder now and shivering, "But- who? Who sent you?"

"That's not important, Evan." He steps over me and walks towards the front gate. He stops and turns to me, "I'll see you in the next, Evan Williams." With that, he turns around and continues forward. His figure getting further and further away.

The cold engulfs my body like a frozen lake I had just fallen through. The darkness pulls me like tar in a pit. I lay there on the threshold of my family home and fight to keep my eyes open. The only comfort I feel is that of the warm breeze on my cold skin and the sickly-sweet smell of the honeysuckle vine swallowing the fence like the darkness swallowing me.

With my final breath, I spit up a combination of words and blood, "In the next."

CHAPTER 13

I sit up in bed quickly as I'm yanked from my sleep, "Benjamin!" I yell.

Memories of a time once forgotten flood my brain and I'm writhing in pain, grasping at a wound on my back that miraculously isn't there. I feel around the sheets of my bed, expecting them to be damp with blood, yet they're dry. I jump out of bed and flip on the light switch. Running over to the mirror, I begin anxiously turning around in the view of it, trying to locate any semblance of a stab wound on my back. The only scars I have are the ones on my side and stomach from when Sam had stabbed me and left me for dead so viciously a few weeks back.

"Leo?" A knock on my door accompanied by Arie's voice, "Are you okay? I heard you yelling."

I hurry over to the door and fling it open. "I know what happened."

She stares at me, wide-eyed. "You don't mean-"

"Yes. I know what happened to me before."

Judging by her face, Arie can hardly believe her ears. "I'll go wake Lydia and Alex. This is great news!"

I look at the clock on the wall in the hallway behind her and see that it's not even five in the morning yet. "No, don't wake them. We can talk about this a little later, when the sun has a chance to come up. I don't know what I just saw exactly, but I felt it like I was there. I woke up feeling liked I was stabbed."

"Oh honey, you were stabbed, though." She jokes, poking fun at my now-healed punctures.

"Oh, ha ha," I say sarcastically. I roll my eyes, "You're hilarious!"

She laughs and smiles genuinely for the first time in a while. "We can definitely talk about this a little later, but I'm awake now, all thanks to your yelling. Wanna go downstairs and make some coffee?"

"No- I think I'd like to go for a walk. Care to join me?"

Arie looks at me with excited eyes, "Sure. Let me go grab my shoes and I'll meet you downstairs." She heads back to the guest room she had been staying in and I close my door to get dressed.

I put on my bright orange running shoes for the first

time in a long time and stand in front of the mirror again. I lift my shirt to chest level and do a final spin around, double checking to confirm there were no new points of entry on my body. Solidifying the fact that there weren't, I start towards the staircase, pausing at the room Alex was staying in.

Is this the room they were killed in? I wonder to myself. Is this the house? Looking forward, I stop again at the top of the stairs, running my hand along the banister, remembering that this is where I- I mean, Evan- pushed Benjamin over. Running the images through my mind again and again, I can see clearly now that what everyone was talking about was true. This house was my family's home. This is where it all started- the constant death and rebirth. But why? That's the question I intend to find the answer to.

"You coming?" Arie says, already at the bottom of the steps. She's tightening her laces as I descend the nostalgic wooden stairs.

"How long are you willing to walk?" I ask as she stands back up.

"That depends- how long are you gonna be able to keep up?"

I smile and give her a light shoulder bump. "Let's go."

After about an hour and a half of a mix of running and walking- mostly walking for me- I stop on the side of the road overlooking a meadow-like field of green beans just in time to see the sun rise up. I close my eyes and take a few deep breaths as the warmth washes over me, starting on my face and flowing down my body.

From behind closed eyelids, I can see the light shining through my skin, causing a soft orange glow. I stretch my arms out and feel the urge to scream, so I do. I let out a roar of a yell and it feels good. I yell until I feel the air leave my lungs completely and let them fill again, just to empty them a second time.

"What are you doing?" Arie says as she jogs back to my side. "I thought you were in trouble! Scared me half to death, asshole!" She punches my bicep and hunches over, breathing heavily.

"Sorry- it feels good to get that out, though. You should try it," I say, gesturing at the open field.

She turns her head to look up at me, then raises her arm out, pointing at the field. "You want me to yell at some green beans?"

Laughing, I say, "Yes. I want you to yell at some green beans with me. Trust me- it feels good."

Without a second guess, Arie faces the field and screams at the sun. She screams longer than I could, thanks to her iron lungs and pauses only to take in more breath. I fill my lungs and yell with her again before we both turn our yells into laughter and hug each other.

"Felt good, didn't it?" I ask as we approach the gate out front of the house.

"It did. It really did." She smiles at me as she walks past the vines growing along the fence.

"You know something?" I ask. "These honeysuckle flowers haven't bloomed once these last couple of weeks- but here they are." I use my fingers and delicately pluck one from the vine. Puling the stem from the flower, I collect the sweet drop of nectar on my tongue. More memories of garden parties and being chased by my mother around the garden flood my head and I fall to my knees, sobbing.

"Oh, Leo." Arie says as she drops to my side and cradles me in her arms. "It's gonna be okay."

I begin crying too hard to speak, only remembering and feeling emotions of a past life. The memories aren't necessarily mine, but the feelings are all too real. I cry for the life I lived before with the parents who loved me and the goals I never got to accomplish. Mostly, though, I cry for the child who could do nothing to save himself.

That all changes now, I think to myself. I'm coming for you Sam- Benjamin- whatever the fuck your name is.

After my shower, I decide to make breakfast for the house. With four of us here in total, I figure I better get a head's start before they all wake up and I have the opportunity to inform them of my revelation. I start with brewing a full carafe of coffee- a full bodied, dark roast that sends nodes of chocolate and cherry throughout the first floor.

Next, while the coffee is brewing, I get started on some French toast. It's been years since I'd had French toast and today seems like the perfect day for it. While the brioche bread is swimming in a couple of beat eggs, vanilla extract, and cinnamon, I work on making a blueberry compote for a topping.

The smells are waltzing together throughout the house and I can hear stirring in the rooms above my head. Lydia opens her bedroom door down the hall from the kitchen and I see her moments later standing in the doorway, rubbing her eyes.

"Is that French toast?" She asks with a wide smile.

"Sure is! I also just brewed a fresh pot of coffee. Help yourself to a cup while I finish this up." I say, handing her one of the mugs I had already taken out of the cupboard in preparation.

Pouring herself a full mug of liquid black gold, she asks, "What's all this for?"

"We'll go over all that in a bit. For now, take a seat. Would you like bacon, scrapple, or both?" I reply, all but brushing off her question.

"I'll have both!" She says greedily.

Just as I finish up plating Lydia's breakfast, Arie and Alex come down the hall with hungry expressions.

"Yes, bro! I love your French toast!" Alex exclaims, bringing back memories of when we still lived at home with mom and dad. I would make breakfast most mornings because our parents couldn't be bothered.

Shaking off the memories of a darker time, I pass Alex his plate and tell him to sit as well. Arie grabs a mug of coffee and a few pieces of bacon before she sits down in between the two of them.

"Okay, so are you going to tell us now?" Lydia asks, crunching on the last few pieces of her bacon.

"Yes, right." I start, "I think I understand it all now."

Alex sits his fork down, "So you're saying you remember it all now?"

All three of them look at me and Arie smiles, already aware of what I'm about to say.

"Yes. I remember- not all of it so far, but enough. I remembered how I died the first time. It was here, in this very house. How is that possible?"

Lydia sits up in her chair, "That's because this is your house, Leo. Well- it was your old family's house. The Williams Family owned this house up until the three of them were murdered by Benjamin Samuel Crane in the late 1800's. Benjamin, today, is Sam. See the connection in the name? My old family, the Greenes, inherited the house upon the death of the original owners. In my old life, I was the Williams's housekeeper. When I was fired, I left town for a while. I had to figure out my life and find out what I wanted to do with it.

It was only after the death of the three of them that my brother, Henry," she motions towards Alex, "wrote me a letter explaining what had happened and how in his will, Mr. Williams stated that, 'In the event of the end of the Williams's bloodline, the estate will be inherited by the trusted Greene family, with whom their service remained longest with the Williams family.'"

"So when my family died, your family took over the estate?" I asked, sipping my coffee.

"Precisely. And here it has been ever since. I've made minor updates, but I had always strived to keep the layout as identical as possible to the original manor in case it would ever help jog your memory."

"So that's why you sleep downstairs?"

"Yes- I sleep downstairs in the room that I used to call my own. It feels more natural that way."

Nodding my head, I'm starting to make sense of things. Lydia sleeps in her old room; the parlor déjà vu I've experienced; the memories of the foyer and the garden-everything is making perfect sense as to why it all feels so familiar.

"I had high hopes that you'd remember much earlier on when you chose to stay in your old room upstairs. When it didn't happen, I called Arie to come stay with us, thinking maybe she could find out a way to help you remember."

"So who were you in the old life?" I ask, turning directly towards Arie. "How do you fit in?"

"Funny story, actually," she starts. "Benjamin Crane was my brother."

Silence falls over the room as I realize this whole time that at any given time, I haven't been as safe as I thought I was. My pulse starts beating in my eyes and I have to grip the counter to hold myself up as my knees go weak.

"It's okay, Leo." Alex says. "You can trust her."

"How? How can I trust the person who's probably leading Sam here as we speak?" I'm furious now, my hands are shaking uncontrollably.

Arie starts, "Leo, it isn't like that. Ben-"

"Stop talking for a second. I need to think."

"Leo, Arie is trying to tell you-" Lydia says.

How could she defend Arie?

"Trying to tell me what exactly?"

Arie continues calmly, “I’m trying to tell you that Benjamin killed me too. Believe me when I say-”

I interject, “Believe you? You want me to believe you? This whole time I thought you were my best friend, but now it just feels like you got close to me for Sam. What the actual fuck is going on here? Did you really think I wouldn’t catch on?”

“Stop being an ass, Leo.” Alex says curtly. “Let her explain before you say something you might regret.”

He looks at me seriously and his words are enough to silence me- for now, at least. I roll my eyes and wave my hands, urging Arie to hurry up and get to the point.

“Believe me when I say, I know the feeling of betrayal you’re feeling right now. Benjamin was a great brother growing up. He cared deeply for our family. When our mother died, something inside him changed. He never wanted to come around anymore. Any chance he had, he would escape to the barn my family owned.

None of that seemed concerning until we started noticing chickens disappearing. One by one, they would be gone. It was one a week, and then one every other day. As quick as we were replacing them, they were vanishing.

So one night, I watched from my window as Benjamin walked into the barn through one door and out through the back door, in the direction of the forest.”

“What does this have to do with anything?” I interrupt.

"I'm getting there." She replies. "I decided to follow him because I saw him with a chicken in his arms. Keeping my distance, I followed him into the woods and eventually he came upon a clearing where I watched him cut the chicken's head off and watch as it bled out. There was someone else there that night, but it was dark so I couldn't make out a face under the hood. When I couldn't make sense of what was happening, I decided to go home and tell my father.

I must have stepped on a twig or something, because a crunch sound alerted him to my position. He called out my name, but I started running away. I heard him chasing after me and with how much larger he was then me, he caught up pretty quickly." Her eyes start filling with tears and Lydia grabs her hand while Alex rubs her back.

"I struggled trying to fight him off of me, but before I could break free of his grasp, the world felt cold. My brother, who used to care so much about our family, had murdered me in cold blood. Then, strangely, I woke up again as if nothing had ever happened. Only this time-things were different. Times changed and none of us looked the same."

"So we were all reborn?" I ask, completely blown away by the story laid out before me.

"Well that was the first time. I have died and come back

at least four times now. Each time I was killed by someone I'm assuming was a different version of Benjamin."

"So far, that's the only connection we all share with each other." Lydia continues, "Aside from the constant death and rebirth, each one of us was murdered by some version of Benjamin. Our running theory is if one of us manages to kill him first this time, it'll break the cycle. That "one of us" being you, Leo."

"Me? Why do I have to?" Shocked by what Lydia is suggesting, I suddenly feel nauseous.

"Because you're the one who managed to get closest to him in each life. If anyone knows a weakness, it's you." Alex jumps in. "At least, that's another theory of ours." He shrugs his shoulders as if he didn't just drop yet another bomb on me.

I lean onto the countertop of the kitchen island we're all surrounding with our breakfasts now long cold. I rub my temples to alleviate the sudden pressure building behind my forehead.

"How do you propose we do this, then?" I ask, shocking the three of them with my willingness to get right to it. "How do I end this for all of us?"

Alex shifts on his barstool, "Well bro, now we gotta find your mom."

CHAPTER 14

A couple of days after my failed French toast breakfast, Alex and Lydia were finally able to track down a woman named Wendy Haverford, whom they claim to be my "old mother." Once he was off the phone with the woman's daughter, Alex looked at Lydia, shook his head, and hung his head low.

"Damn it!" Lydia starts pacing back and forth in the parlor. "What do we do now?"

"What happened?" I ask quietly.

Alex sits down after pouring a glass of the good scotch, "I don't know, Lydia. This was the only lead we had and the only plan we made up."

"What happened?" I ask again since the both of them ignored me.

Lydia looks at me, defeated, "Your mother is dead, Leo. It seems like Sam got to her first."

"How could this have happened? How did she die?" Arie asks, surprised at the news.

Alex explains, "Her daughter said she was checking the mailbox at the end of her driveway when a car came out of nowhere and ran her down. She said the same car backed up over her, then drove forward again before taking off down the street." He takes a sip of his drink. "She said she saw the whole thing. That was two days ago."

"Oh my God, that's awful!" Arie sinks into the couch cushions. "What do we do now? He's probably on his way here now."

"Don't panic, Arie. We just need another plan. Any ideas?" Lydia's gaze bounces off each of us. "Anyone?"

"We wait for him to come to us." Everyone's eyes dart to me in unison.

"No. That doesn't work for me." Alex finishes his drink and starts pouring another. "We're sitting ducks. You expect us to wait for him to come to us- just so he can potentially kill all of us again?"

Shaking her head, Lydia continues, "Yeah, I'm with Alex. That doesn't seem like the best course of action."

"Well we don't really have another choice, do we? I'm tired of hiding and constantly looking over my shoulder. I'm ready to finish this. I want my life to go back to normal and I know it won't ever be normal again, but getting rid of the ghost that haunts us is a damned good start."

All three of them sit up a little straighter and I can tell they're focusing on what I'm saying, considering it even.

"We need him to come here, that much is true. We can't obviously go to him- we don't know where he's hiding. And any public place is off limits. He only tried to kill me because he didn't think anyone else was around. So- we do it here. We end it where it all began."

Feeling proud of myself for giving a superhero's speech right before the squad defeats the bad guy, my pride is cut down to size when Lydia starts laughing.

"I'm sorry- I don't mean to laugh, but how do you propose we get Sam to come here? Are we just gonna text him?" She says questioningly. "I think you forgot- the police found his phone at the scene. There isn't a sound way to actually get ahold of this guy, let alone bring him into my house."

"Maybe- maybe not. We can use me as bait." I say, considering my options.

All at once, the parlor is overcome by voices pleading me not to be so stupid and the sound of everyone saying 'no.'

"I'm not asking for permission here, guys. In case you haven't noticed, he's already onto us. If he's the one that killed my mother, then he somehow knew we were onto him. We need to end this before any more of us get killed again."

"What's the plan?" Arie says, causing the three of us to look at her in amazement.

"Well I already know he's watching me." I admit. "When we were at the cafe the other day, I felt like someone was watching me. I thought I saw him in a parked car across the street, but when you guys pulled me into the conversation, I looked again and didn't see him anymore. I wrote it off as just a random someone sitting in their car, but ever since that day, I can't shake the feeling that he's watching- waiting for me to be alone here.

So we make it happen. The three of you need to leave, but not in an obvious way. What I'm thinking is- Arie and Lydia leave together in one car, but make it seem like you're going to the store or something. Take some shopping bags with you.

Alex, you need to leave separately. Sam knows that you're my estranged brother. If he really has been watching like I'm confident he has, then he'll probably think you came for a couple days just to see how I'm doing."

"This is crazy, you know that?" Lydia asks with her hands on her hips. "You're gonna be left alone and for how long?"

"Yeah, bro- I don't like it. Not one bit." Shaking his head, Alex stands up and finishes his second drink. "But I trust you." He smiles and walks towards the stairs, stopping to grab my shoulder.

"Thank you, Alex." I say, looking up at him.

Nodding in agreement, Arie heads upstairs with him to get ready. I turn to Lydia, who's now staring out of the parlor windows, seemingly scanning the yard for any possible sign of my killer ex-boyfriend.

"Lydia- I just want you to know- I appreciate everything you did for me. If I make it out of here alive-"

"Not if- when. You need to beat him, Leo. Not just for us, but for you." She walks past me and into her room to get ready.

Scanning the front yard, I catch a glimpse of what I think is someone in the woods beyond the fence, but blink and lose sight of them. I decide to start a fire in the fireplace and pour myself a glass of scotch for *literal* old time's sake. I'm about to sit down when Arie and Alex come from upstairs carrying their jackets and wearing their shoes.

Alex confirms he has his car keys and his phone in case I need him- Arie does the same. We hug each other for a while, promising this isn't goodbye. Lydia comes out of her room and hugs me quickly, walking past the three of us and out the front door.

"Pay her no mind- she's pretty stubborn." Alex jokes as he lightly punches my chest. "Good luck, bro. We're counting on you." He walks through the open door and gets into his white BMW, which is way louder than any car needs to be.

What a tool, I think to myself and smile.

"Be safe, Leo." Arie says, wiping the tears from her eyes. "Kill that son of a bitch."

I watch as both cars disappear down the driveway and lock the front door immediately after I hear the latch click. I then make my way around to all the windows on the first floor and make sure they're locked as well. I'm making my way upstairs to lock those windows when I hear the floor creak from the far end of the hallway.

Oh good- he's already inside. My heart starts racing.

The creak came from the area outside my bedroom door. The window at the end of the hallway must have been how he was able to get inside.

"Sam." I call out from about halfway up the stairs. "I know you're there."

Silence.

"Do we really need to play these games, Sam?" I slowly continue up the stairs, stopping only to text Alex and Lydia: "He's here!"

I reach the top of the staircase and slowly approach the hallway, cautiously peering around the corner. I'm relieved and also slightly disappointed to see that no one is standing there and the window is still closed. Was the creak sound in my imagination? Just my mind playing tricks on me?

I shake it off and lock that window first. Then I make my way into my room and one by one lock the windows in the upstairs bedrooms on my way to the stairs. The final room I still have to secure is the room my old parents were murdered in. I take a deep breath and turn the doorknob.

When I open the door, I notice the window is open. I glance around the room and see no one, so I figure the coast is clear. I walk to the window and notice the broken glass strewn about the carpet underneath of it. Upon further inspection, I realize the window isn't just open- it's broken. Footsteps behind me cause me to hesitate before I turn around.

"Hi, Leo," A familiar voice says before slamming his fist into the side of my face.

I slowly open my eyes and realize I'm now in the dining room downstairs, tied to a dining chair. Sam sits at the other end of the table from me, eating leftovers from the night before. He looks up at me after he takes a couple bites and smiles, wiping his mouth with the corner of a paper towel.

"Ah, there he is!" He yells, joyfully. "How was the nap? You were out like a light, you know that?"

"Fuck you."

"Well that's not nice for the host to say. Do you treat all your guests like this?" He says, taking another bite.

"I already texted Lydia. She knows you're here. They'll be home any second."

He puts his fork down and wipes his mouth again, laughing. "Well wouldn't that be swell? Oh wait- it's not gonna happen. I texted her too. Told her to stay out until the coast was clear. By coast I mean you and by clear, I mean dead."

"What are you talking about?"

"God- I must have really knocked the sense out of you, huh? Or are you just plain fucking stupid, Leo? Think!" He yells. "Who do you think gave me the green light? Yeah, I've been watching you. But I haven't done anything because Lydia wanted me to make it look like a coincidence."

"No- that-"

"Yes. I get it- don't believe me. I swear on your mom I'm not lying." He sucks his teeth, "yikes. Sorry- was that insensitive? Considering the fact that she's dead again?" He laughs again, slapping the table with his palm. "I really crack myself up."

I have no words to say to him, so I sit there in silence,

trying to think of how his story makes sense. My mind flashes to all the times Lydia disappears to her room to answer the phone. It flashes to the time I overheard her conversation with "Arie." No. It can't be true.

"Cat got your tongue?" He says, finishing his last bite. "You know what? You're bitter. I get it. It's always awkward running into your ex." He rolls his eyes. "Tell you what, Leo- I'm gonna go see if there's any dessert in this shit-hole. Might even pour myself some of that good wine. Want some?"

"Fuck. You." I say through gritting teeth. "You won't get away with this, Sam."

"Oh, baby, I already have. Once I'm done with you, we'll get rid of the other two and hell- I might even kill Lydia just for fun. You must have really pissed her off, you know that? Again- not like it even matters. I'll kill you and all your little friends." He kneels next to me with a hand on the bank of my neck. "Then I'm gonna burn this fucking house to the ground. Lydia will just come back and rebuild or whatever the fuck she does every time. You know she used to be good. She used to be a fighter.

I don't know what changed this time, but she switched sides. Too bad it doesn't matter anymore. The bitch is weak. I personally think she only tells me what I wanna hear so I don't kill her. HA!" He laughs in my ear so loudly I feel my eardrum almost rupture.

I sit there, unable to grasp my ear, writhing in pain while he laughs his way to the kitchen to do as he said. Once the pain subsides a bit, I try to wiggle one of my hands free and to my surprise, I'm able to loosen the bindings around both wrists.

I manage to pull both hands out of the wraps and leave them clasped behind me to maintain appearances. I'm constantly scanning the room for something to use as a weapon when I look in front of me and see his dinnerware on the other end of the table. The son of a bitch never was good at cleaning up after himself. God- what did I see in him?

"No dessert, but some really good fucking wine. Think Lydia will mind?" Sam says as he enters the room with the bottle in one hand and a full glass in the other.

I don't reply.

"Eh- you're probably right." He places the bottle on the table and leans on the edge in front of me. "Would you like some?"

"No- but you should have more!" I grab the bottle quick and smash it across his head, knocking him to the floor unconscious.

While he's lying there, I begin untying the bindings around my waste and my ankles and finally manage to get free when I notice Sam stirring out of the corner of my eye.

He lets out a groan as I run past him towards the

staircase, "Ugh. What the fuck did you do to me?" Standing now, he starts after me, regaining his bearings.

I'm halfway up the stairs when he makes it to the foyer. Looking up at me, he slowly walks to the bottom of the stairs. Then, with a burst of what I'm assuming is adrenaline, he starts skipping steps on his way up.

I'm barely around the corner into the hallway when he lunges from the top of the steps and tackles me to the floor. I hit my head hard and my vision starts going in and out with each heartbeat. He sits on me, straddling my thighs and forces my hands under his knees. Pulling out a small pocketknife, he starts sliding it across my face, sharp side facing away.

"Say you love me, baby." He says, holding my face in one hand, the knife in the other.

"Fuck you!" I yell, spitting in his face.

Wiping his mouth, he slaps me hard across the face then makes an incision on my chin with his knife.

"Look what you made me do, Leo!" He drops the knife and puts both hands around my throat, squeezing tightly.

I'm choking out the words, "Stop. Please!"

It doesn't matter how much a protest- Sam wants me dead. He squeezes harder and harder and I can feel my throat collapsing. The tightness and lack of oxygen starts causing me to blackout and finally he lets go and stands up. Looking down at me, he unbuttons his pants.

"I should get one more use out of you before you die, huh? While you're still cute anyway." He starts to pull out his dick when the doorbell rings. "Who is it?" He yells, walking towards the banister, looking down at the front door from the balcony.

I slowly regain the strength to sit up and I try my best to remain as silent as possible as I make my way towards him on all fours, evenly spreading my weight to avoid the creaky old floorboards.

A muffled voice yells out, "It's Alex! Leo's brother."

"Oh, hey man! I'll be right down!" Sam shouts back. Turning around, "Guess your brother wants in on-" He makes eye contact with me and chokes on his words. "Leo, what the fuck are you doing?"

I smile at him, "Ending it."

And with the hardest decision I've ever had to make, I ended the plague that was engulfing my entire life. With one simple push, it felt like my life started anew.

"Finally." I inhaled while a single tear hurried down my cheek, the saltiness burning the fresh gash once it reaches my chin. Breathing out, "I'm finally free."

Thud.

I look over the railing and see his eyes staring up at me at the same time the front door gets kicked in by Alex.

"Leo!" His eyes shoot from Sam to me. "You did it!"

"Where's Lydia?" I ask.

"She didn't come back yet?"

"No- and I think Arie's in trouble."

"What do you mean she's in trouble?" Alex asks, worried expression on his face. "In what way?"

"Alex, Lydia is the one behind all of this."

Alex's face runs flush and his stare is blank for a few seconds. In those few, agonizing seconds, my mind races to think of where Lydia could possibly have gone with Arie.

"If Lydia is the one behind this, why was Sam the one trying to kill you? If this was all Lydia, why didn't she just kill you the first night you stayed here? Or when she found you in the park?"

I shrug my shoulders, "I have no idea yet. I fully intend to find out, though. First, we have to figure out what to do about Sam's body." I gesture towards my ex, face-up on the table in the center of the room.

"Are we sure that he's actually dead, though? People can definitely survive a fall from that height." Alex says, rubbing the back of his neck anxiously. "Should we check for a pulse?"

"I'll check- just to be sure." I slowly approach Sam, half expecting him to jump up and stab me in the chest or snap my neck. Giving myself goosebumps, I reach both my index and middle fingers towards his jugular to feel for any sign of life still inside this empty husk before me. When my fingers make contact with his throat, I let out a sigh of relief. Nothing. I run my fingers along his eyelids to close them.

"He's gone," I manage to say over choked words.

I bow my head and can feel the weight of the events this evening fall upon my shoulders. I sink to my knees next to Sam's lifeless body and start to cry. Everything is fucked. My boyfriend tried to kill me, but I killed him instead. I killed him- me. I physically ended his life and now reality seems so altered that I feel like any second, I'm going to wake up from one big, long nightmare.

Instead, a hand grasps my shoulder and I tilt my head to meet Alex's sorrowful eyes. I grab hold of his hand and cry harder. Everything has changed. I'll never tell Sam I love him again. I'll never hear his laugh when we're watching a funny stand-up special on Netflix. I'll never feel the love he made me feel ever again.

Sure, the whole relationship was a lie to get close to me, but regardless, he was still my first love. I can't ever forget the times we had because they truly felt genuine. I can't go on in life thinking that each part was an act. I refuse to believe that not one single part of Sam's love for me was pure. It couldn't have all been fake, right?

An hour or so after my breakdown, all I feel is anger, sadness, and pain. I want revenge. I want Arie back. I want this whole thing to be behind me once and for all.

"Are you sure you want to do this, Leo?" Alex asks, holding the empty gas can.

Pulling out a pack of matches I swiped from the mantle in the parlor, I reply, "Yeah, I'm sure. This house holds nothing but bad memories and I'm ready to move on from this place." I take a look one last time up at the balcony in the foyer and my mind flashes to images of my mom and dad looking down at me, smiles on their faces as my father stands beside my mother, both of them seemingly accepting this is the last time we'd see each other.

I look back at Sam's body, still stationary on the table in front of me. I bend over and kiss his forehead lightly, rubbing his cheek with my thumb. He smells heavily of gasoline, thanks to Alex dousing pretty much the entire first level of my childhood home in the stuff.

"I'll be outside, Leo." Alex sits the gas can down next to the table and walks out to the car.

I stand up and take one last stroll through the hallway into the kitchen and walk over to the stove. I turn on the gas and head toward the exit, stopping once more in the doorway to the parlor. My mind flashes yet again to when I first met Benjamin and heard my parents and him laugh together for the first time.

I smile and walk through the threshold of the front door, out onto the porch. Turning around, I grab a match from the booklet and strike it on the railing outside. Holding the tiny flame in front of my face, I look back at Sam, one last time.

"I love you, Sam." I whisper, tears in my eyes. "I'll see you in the next."

I toss the match into the foyer and watch as the flames quickly roar across the wooden floor, engulfing everything in their path. I pull the door closed and head down the front porch steps towards Alex's car, which had already been started. The glow from the flames in the windows grows brighter on the driveway and I can see the illumination spread across the dash as I buckle my seatbelt.

"Where to next, bro?" Alex says, trying too hard to sound cool.

"Anywhere but here, "bro,"" I say with a smirk.

Alex chuckles, his cheeks turning a slight pink. He grabs the gear shift and switches the car into drive. I watch the house from the passenger side mirror as the flames have now spread to the second story. The house gets smaller and smaller in the mirror and I shut my eyes, allowing the sleep to take over. Exhaustion creeps in and wrestles with body aches and bruises and before we leave the driveway, I'm fast asleep.

CHAPTER 15

It didn't take long for the blaze of my childhood home to be noticed and reported. Within minutes, an armada of fire trucks, police cruisers, and paramedics arrived on the scene to extinguish the fire of whatever was left. By the time they all got there, however, little was left of the Victorian home, aside from the honeysuckle growing on the fence and parts of the wrap around porch.

Alex and I had been long gone by the time the fearless first responders showed up at the scene- I made sure of that. That was about a week ago. Now, Alex and I were on the verge of finding Lydia and Arie. After days of searching, we tracked them west, towards California. It would only be a matter of time before we crossed paths with them and we were hopeful.

For someone so planned out, Lydia was being sloppy on the run. Instead of using cash, she still proceeds to use her credit cards for gas and lodging. Each time we track her to a new motel, her and Arie are already long gone. This most recent time we were almost right on top of them, it seems. The hair dryer in the bathroom was still slightly warm to the touch, meaning we had just missed them.

With each location, it feels like we take two steps towards Lydia and Arie, while they take three. Sooner or later, we'd have to step on their toes, right?

"We're so close I can feel it." Alex says, gripping the steering wheel harder, albeit excitedly.

"We can't let our guard down. She's still dangerous. We don't even know if Arie is still alive at this point. If we find them, we need to be smart about how we approach them. I'm not taking any chances this time. The bitch is going to pay for what she did."

Alex's smile fades to a stony expression. "Right. She's tricked us before, so I don't see why she wouldn't again. Only this time- she'd be like a cornered animal."

"Exactly." I say, nodding my head. "How about we stop off at the next rest stop and switch? You've been driving all night."

"That would be lovely." He says, looking at me with tired eyes and dark circles deep enough to grow roots.

A few minutes later we see a sign for "Rest Stop: Next

Exit" and get off when prompted. We pick a spot up front, near the entrance of the building and get out to stretch before checking out the vending machines and using the restrooms. I stop when I get out of the car and think of my last adventure in a rest stop. This time, though, I have back up should anything go down unexpectedly.

The sun is starting to peak over the tops of the trees surrounding the parking lot and the early morning fog sits thinly atop the grass around the building and empty picnic tables. Walking toward the vending machine area, I decide a Honeybun would make a perfect breakfast snack and notice one of those automatic coffee makers tucked away in the corner. I scrunch my face at the thought of the horribly burned coffee flavor mixed with the essence of the Styrofoam cup and decide something is better than nothing.

As the coffee maker screeches to life, spitting out the sad excuse of brown water that the company likes to call 'A Convenient Cup O' Joe,' I scan my surrounding outside of the vending area. Aside from our car, a random Suburban and Mini Coop are among the only other cars in the parking lot, both of which have those cheap windshield mesh covers to block out the sunlight and I can hear the low sound of their engines running for air circulation while the inhabitants sleep soundly.

Alex exits the restroom and makes his way towards me, "Mm, coffee! I could use a cup, too!"

I offer up my cup, deciding that nothing, in fact, is better than something. I think back to about ten minutes ago when we passed a sign for a Starbucks and contemplate whether it'd be worth it to backtrack our trip a little bit for a more convenient cup of Joe.

"God! This is awful!" Alex says, swallowing a mouthful of the scalding hot brown water. "Why is this a thing?"

I laugh and tell him about the Starbucks down the road. Almost immediately, he tosses the cup of coffee into the garbage and swirls his finger the air, "Let's go!"

Pulling out of the drive-through, I look over at Alex, who's cradling a latte in his hands like it's a small puppy.

"Better?" I ask, already knowing the answer to my question.

"Much better!" He says, taking a sip from his cup. "I'm so glad we stopped."

"Me too- especially if I have to drive all day. I need the extra energy." Merging onto the highway, I turn up the radio just enough to hear a little background noise aside from the tiny sips Alex is taking from his cup.

"So what happens when we find them?" Alex asks the inevitable question. "What are you going to do?"

I pause and think on his question for a little bit. What will I do? What's going to happen when I see the woman who almost single handedly is to blame for turning my entire life upside down?

It's been a week since I found out Lydia betrayed all of us. In that those seven days, she's had Arie held hostage as they drive around the country trying to get away. Leads go dead as we just barely land on top of them and with each let down, it only adds fuel to the fire burning inside of me.

"Honestly, I have no idea. A huge part of me wants to hurt her- maybe even kill her, but will that actually end this? We thought that if I killed Sam, it would break whatever fucked up reincarnation cycle we're all a part of. Then again- that's exactly what Lydia told us, so who knows? Maybe we're just destined to keep coming back and killing each other over and over again for all eternity."

"That's messed up, Leo- a little too dark for this early in the morning."

"Well, my life is pretty dark right now. I just found out I was living with a nut job who kidnapped my best friend, then I killed my boyfriend. The future seems a little bleak. Forgive me for being a little honest."

"Listen, we're going to find Arie. Maybe while we're at it, we'll figure out what's going on with that fucked up cycle. For now, though, I think you need to be a little easier on yourself, bro. You've been through a lot this last year. You're a survivor- that much is true. At least you're not alone."

I look over at him with a puzzling look on my face, "How so?"

"I mean- think about it. Who hasn't had a crazy ex? Remember Christine? Total nut job."

I laugh out loud as I remember his ex-fiancée and how she would show up at his job accusing him of cheating and then turn up at family dinners when she wasn't invited.

"Okay, so maybe you do understand a little bit!" We laugh together for a little while and it feels good. I haven't had a good laugh in a long time and it's nice to be close to someone who isn't trying to kill me for a change.

Eventually, the laughs get quieter and I look over at my older brother, whose eyelids are weighing heavily on his eyes, despite the extra shot of espresso he ordered. He adjusts in his seat to try and stay awake.

"Why don't you put the seat back and rest? You drove all night- I'm sure you're tired." I ask, motioning towards the lever on his seat.

"Yeah, I think I just need a little shut eye. I'm no good if I'm tired and can't keep up when you're chasing that psycho once we find her." He puts his empty latte cup in the coffee holder and tilts his seat back as far as it goes. Within seconds, he's already asleep with his mouth open and his eyes dancing behind his eyelids.

I turn the radio up a few notches so I can hear a little more, but not enough to disturb Alex. My eyes dart from overhead sign to overhead sign on the highway headed west.

I will find you, Arie. Just hang in there.

My mind starts shuffling through scenarios of what will happen when we find them and I have to shake my head to stop thinking about it. Most of them are dark. They almost always end with someone dying. But I'll cross that bridge when I get to it. For now, I have about 500 miles left before I'm in Santa Barbara and I don't plan on stopping for anything else except gas. *See you soon, Lydia.*

CHAPTER 16

When we finally get to Santa Barbara, we stop at the first hotel we come across. We both have been taking turns driving while the other sleeps since we left New York, so the both of us are absolutely exhausted. It also doesn't help that it's been drizzling since we crossed the city line- a bad omen, perhaps?

"Let's stay here for the night and rest. First thing tomorrow we can start looking for the girls." Alex says groggily. "I can hardly keep my eyes open anymore."

"Sounds like a plan. I need a nice, hot shower and a good firm pillow," I say while daydreaming.

I park the car under the awning outside of the entrance and head inside. As soon as the automatic doors slide open, I'm greeted by the soft sounds of piano music from the speakers in the ceiling and the smile of a man so unbelievably handsome, I blush almost instantly.

"Hi there! How can I help you this evening?" He says so warmly and welcoming that my heart melts inside my chest.

"Hello! I'd like to rent a couple of rooms for two nights, if that's okay!" If that's okay? It's a fucking hotel, you idiot.

"It'd be my pleasure." He says, flashing his beautiful smile. Now that I'm closer, I take note of the caramel-colored skin flowing from underneath his suit. His undershirt is unbuttoned lower than the dress code probably allows, but I'm seeing no reason to complain.

His chest is well-defined and pulling the highest buttons apart. The chiseled line that runs down the center of his torso is so tempting I have to fight the urge to reach across the desk and catch a harassment lawsuit. Instead, I undress him with my eyes and trace the the outlines of his waist down to his-

"Will that be alright?" He asks, catching me off-guard. His eyes looking at me, one eyebrow tilted and a slight smirk on his diamond-cut face.

Embarrassed, I manage to spit out a quick, "Yes!" Yes what?

"Wonderful!" His eyes linger on me a little longer than they should and I feel a palpitation. "So two queen rooms across the hall from one another. If you'd like to take a seat, I'll just be another minute or two and we'll get you all settled in." His hand extends toward the lobby full of open chairs.

I nod and walk towards the chairs, hoping that his gaze would follow me along the way. As I turn around, I notice his eyes lock with mine and he smiles slightly with wanting eyes. I've played this game, buddy. You just wandered into my mousetrap. I smile back at him and look away, pretending to be uninterested.

Suddenly, my phone vibrates and I remember I have a brother in the car. Putting the phone up to my ear, "Hello?"

"Uh- hello? Are we checked in or what?" Alex says, more exhausted than annoyed- even though he sounded pretty annoyed with me for leaving him in the car.

"Yeah, he's finishing up with the booking now. It shouldn't be much longer."

"Okay, great. Don't forget I'm out here! It's easy to lose track of time when you're eye-fucking the concierge." He chuckles and I look out the lobby windows and into the passenger side of the car parked outside the main entrance to see Alex waving and laughing. I wave back and turn my gesture into a lone middle finger while hanging up with the other hand.

As I put my phone in my back pocket, I hear footsteps and look up in time to see the concierge headed my way with keycards and paperwork for me to sign. When I wonder if he had seen the obscene gestures my brother and I just exchanged like kids, his expression tells me that he in fact had.

"I must apologize, Mr. Daniels. I should've asked if you and your guest would have liked a single room instead of two. Give me a moment and-"

"Oh, don't even worry about it-" My eyes scan his name tag after taking a quick glance at the map of his chest once again- "Adam. That's my brother. I am, in fact, single as fuck." Shocked that I had just said that out loud, I gasp and sit up straighter. My face starts burning hot with humiliation and Adam laughs.

"Well that's shocking to hear." He laughs and looks in my direction with a twinkle in his eyes.

We lock eyes for a bit, and I keep finding new things to be attracted to. His eyes are honey-brown and perfectly accent his light-skinned complexion. I could absolutely get lost in his trance, but then he clears in throat and ruins the moment it felt like we were having.

"So," he starts, "These forms are liability waivers and all that fun stuff. We have amenities that are available at no extra charge, continental breakfast, a gym, and more. Lobby is open twenty-four seven and there will always be someone available if you have questions or need room service."

I nod and sign away as he continues talking about the

boring stuff. “Do you think I’d be able to get a tour?” I say when he pauses to let me sign the last couple of pages.

“I’m sure I can arrange something.” He meets my gaze and his eyes move down to my lips. “Let’s get you settled in first. When you and your brother are settled, feel free to come get me and I’ll show the two of you around.”

A little disappointed that Alex may want to come with us, I nod my head again and hand Adam my credit card. I watch him gather the forms and my card and take it back to the desk. A few minutes later, he walks back to me with my card in his hand and a business card with his name on it. I read, Adam Hilliard, General Manager.

Not just a concierge, then. I smile and look back up at him. “I’ll be back for that tour, Adam.”

“I look forward to it, Mr. Daniels.” He says, smiling yet again. I don’t think I’ll ever get over that smile.

“Leo. Call me Leo.”

“I look forward to it, Leo.”

After Alex and I lug our suitcases and belongings to the fourth floor of the hotel, we disappear into our respective rooms. Alex is desperate for any type of slumber that doesn’t involve a stiff passenger car seat and I’m desperately fishing through my luggage trying to find a razor to clean up a bit before my tour with Adam.

It's been so long since I've been intimate with someone that I kind of let my pubic hair do its own thing these last couple of weeks. Am I that desperate to get a potential amount of action that I'd shave at the first possibility of getting fucked? Yes. Yes, I am.

Cleaning up doesn't take as long as I anticipated it would and before I know it, I'm picking out clothes to wear like it's my first date. I decide to play it cool with a pair of distressed, light blue jeans with white sneakers and a Dodgers jersey, which seems to be my favorite outfit at the moment. I skip the underwear because I decide none of the pairs I brought are sexy enough to be ripped off so it would mean easier access for whoever was willing to enter me.

Stopping to look at myself in the mirror first, I decide to unbutton the top button of my jersey, exposing a little bit of my chest. I perform a twist in the mirror to take a look at how my butt looks in these jeans and decide I look good enough to eat.

The elevator dings once it reaches the ground level and the doors slide open. I make my way toward the lobby and see Adam typing at his computer; the soft glow of the screen shining up at him. He must see me out of the corner of his eye, because he looks up at me and smiles before I'm halfway across the lobby.

"Ready for the tour, Leo?" He asks, turning off the computer screen in front of him, while looking at me up and down.

"I sure am!" I say, trying to sound more enthusiastic than attention starved. "Where to first?"

"I can show you the pool and then the gym. After that, we can take a stroll and I'll show you a few stops along the way."

We make our way down the hallway, past the elevator and through a set of double doors. The indoor pool is empty this time of night, so naturally it's quiet and smells like fresh chlorine.

"This is our Olympic-sized swimming pool. It usually doesn't get too crowded throughout the day, so sometimes I like to sneak here on my days off and get a few laps in. You seem like you like to exercise too, so I wouldn't be surprised to see you in here out-swimming me!" He says and lightly squeezes my shoulder. My knees go weak when he touches me and thankfully, I don't collapse in front of him. "Speaking of exercise- let's make our way to the gym."

He holds the door for me and I can't help but to think that long-dead chivalry had been revived in that moment. We make our way back down the hall, and round a corner when I see the sign for the gym.

"Here's the gym. It's also open all hours of the day and like the pool, it's use at your own risk. We don't have a lifeguard or a personal trainer on duty, so if you use either amenity, please be careful." He catches me checking out his exposed chest and bulging biceps being barely contained by his suit jacket and he smirks.

"I wouldn't mind having you as a workout buddy." I say, heart pounding in my chest. "You could spot me, couldn't you, Adam?" I say, sliding my hands into my back pockets.

"Oh, absolutely. Just say when."

"When."

At that moment, Adam closes the gap between us and pushes me up against the wall, kissing me deeply. He's unbuttoning my jersey while he kisses the skin where my jaw and neck meet. I wrap my arms around his shoulders and quiver at the feeling of his solid body against mine.

I squeeze my hands in between us and start unbuttoning his suit pants, ready to expose the heavy tool he's packing underneath. I'm longing for him to take me from behind right here and now, but just as I feel the warmth of his dick in the palm of my hand, we hear the elevator ding down the hall and he pulls away from me.

"Not here." He says, tucking it back into his pants and adjusting the collar of his undershirt. "Tell you what- I have a break in about an hour. I'll come to you and we can finish what we started."

Defeated, I look down at my exposed midriff, "Okay." I

start buttoning the front of my jersey and look up at Adam, who's already making eye contact with me.

"I'm sorry- I got carried away. I want to. Just not here." He says, straightening his suit jacket before walking back into the hallway, leaving me behind.

I walk to the elevators and hit the call button. I cross my arms as I wait, shame sinking in heavily. What was I thinking? The doors slide open in front of me and instead of walking into the empty chamber, I decide to take the stairs. I slowly make my way up the barren stairwell feeling sorry for myself.

When I get to my room, I realize I had dropped my room key somewhere in the gym and decide to go back down, taking the elevator this time. When I turn around to walk back to the elevator, I hear the latch to my room click open. I spin around to see Adam standing in the doorway, completely naked and fully erect.

"You dropped this, Mr. Daniels." He says with a smile on his face and my room key in his hand. "Oh, and I took my break early. What took you so long?"

I rush over to him, taking his dick in my hand again, this time with a better grip so he can't just pull away.

"I thought I told you my name is Leo," I say, biting my lip seductively.

"My mistake, Leo." He says, closing his eyes in pleasure as I start to stroke him off. "How can I make it up to you?"

"You can give me what I want," I say, backing away from him and dropping my pants just before bending over the bed face down. I turn my head just enough to see the eager look on his face.

"With pleasure." Adam says as he makes his way over to the bed.

The next morning, I wake up to the sound of knocking on my door. I glance at the alarm clock sitting on the nightstand next to my bed and sit up quickly. I rub my eyes and turn to look at Adam, but he's already gone.

Go figure, I think to myself, I finally get laid and it's with someone who wants to hit it and quit it.

"Bro, wake up! We have work to do." I hear Alex's muffled voice behind the closed door. "I grabbed you a blueberry muffin from the breakfast downstairs."

I climb out of bed and grab a robe from the bathroom to wrap around myself seeing as I went to sleep wearing nothing the night before. Did I even get any sleep? As I make my way to the door, I notice a folded piece of paper with my name written on it sitting on the dresser.

Opening the letter, I feel my face widen into a smile as I see a phone number and a name signed, "Adam." He must have left sometime early this morning and didn't want to wake me up.

"Leo! Come on dude. Wake up!"

I unlock the door and open it to find my brother standing there with a muffin in his hands like a peace offering.

"Morning sunshine!" He says. "How'd you sleep? Cause I slept great!"

"I don't think I got much sleep, honestly. But when I did, it was pretty good." I say, biting my lip and smiling to myself as I walk towards the dresser to set the muffin down.

"Oh? Have company over or something?" I turn to see Alex folding his arms and rubbing his chin.

I smile, "You remember the concierge?"

"Oh you dog!" Alex hits me playfully in the bicep. "I had a feeling you guys were giving each other sex eyes."

"Well he was kind enough to leave me his number before he dipped out without saying bye," I say, holding up the note. "Oh- and he's the manager."

"What a gentleman!" Alex says sarcastically and we both laugh. "So are you gonna call him?"

I pause for a second, "What we did last night was a lot of fun, sure. But- I don't see how this could even work out. We live all the way in New York. Plus, I may not even make it out of this situation alive. This was just a chance encounter with a hot guy that will probably never happen again."

"Never know, dude." Alex shrugs his shoulders. "You should call him."

"Maybe. For now, though, I need to shower. Wanna meet me in the lobby in about forty-five?"

"Sure thing. Don't forget about your muffin, either! I had to wrestle it away from a six-year-old."

Rolling my eyes, I say, "Sure you did, wimp." I close the door behind Alex who scoffs at my jab.

Realizing how hungry I actually was, I devour the muffin in record timing. Sucking my fingers clean, I drop the robe and look at myself in the mirror. I take note of the three or four bruises forming on my neck and chest.

I lightly rub my fingers across the dark purple marks and stare back at the note, now unfolded on the bedspread. I start to walk towards it, but decide now isn't a good time. Adam was a great fuck, but there's more important work to be done right now. Shaking my head, I instead walk towards the bathroom to shower and get ready for the day.

When I finish getting ready, I make my way to the hotel lobby to find Alex flirting with the dayshift receptionist.

"Let's go, daddy!" I say in an astonishingly flamboyant tone while grabbing his coat and pulling him towards the exit.

Shaking his head and blushing, he says, "You're an asshole, dude. You know that?"

"Oh calm down! She's into you. See the way she's looking at you?" I nod my head towards the reception area as the lobby doors slowly slide closed. Alex turns to look and holds his hand up as the employee smiles and waves at him like something out of *The Notebook*.

"Okay, good. She's cute, right?"

"She's hot, Alex. Just try not to cream your pants before you even get her into the elevator, deal?" Alex chases me to the car, both of us laughing like we did when we would chase each other as kids. I reach the car first and hop in the driver's seat. Panting when he arrives, Alex sinks into the passenger seat beside me.

"Where to now?" Alex says in between deep breaths.

"Now we find Lydia and Arie and figure out the truth." Suddenly aware of how close we were to finding them after weeks of searching, I relax my body and buckle my seatbelt. "We're so close."

"Leo, what if shit hits the fan?"

"If? Alex, the shit has already been flung around the room at this point. The fan needs to be turned off. I'm going to be the one to end this. I have to be the one to end this."

"I'm saying, what if the situation takes a turn and Arie and I don't make it?"

I turn to look at Alex, who has clear signs of worry strewn about his face from his furrowed brow to his quivering jaw. "Why would you say that? I won't let anything happen to you, dude. You're the only family I have left, Alex. I can't lose any more than I already have. I refuse to."

I lean towards him and pull him into a solid hug. I can feel when he starts sobbing and I ruffle his hair. He wipes his eyes and looks over at me.

"Thanks, Leo. I needed that. I love you, bro." He says, drying his eyes on his sleeve.

"I love you, too. Just trust me, okay?" Alex nods and buckles his seatbelt.

"So where are they?" He asks, straightening in his seat.

Almost on queue two girls walk out of the hotel next door to ours as I turn the key in the ignition and the engine revs to life. "They're close."

"How close?"

"Right under our fucking noses." I point at the girls walking out of the lobby and across the parking lot to the familiar Navigator I'd only just been in myself a couple of weeks ago.

"No way! They were next door to us?" Alex brings his palm to his forehead as he leans on the passenger door. "This whole time?"

I'm in awe of the fact that we got so lucky as to stay in the hotel next door- completely by chance. If we would have known they were next door to us, though, it wouldn't have completely mattered. Alex and I needed rest and while I didn't rest for as long as I should've, I still feel one hundred percent better than I did.

Alex continues, "Should we follow them?" He looks at me inquisitively, eyes wider than they had been all morning.

"I don't think that's a bad idea. But we need to keep our distance. If they see this car, they'll know it's us." My mind starts scouring through ideas. "Or we can stay here and wait for them to get back."

"It's up to you, dude. I'm cool either way."

If we stay, we can plan our next steps, but if we go, we run the risk of the girls noticing us and fleeing, potentially losing them again.

Decidedly, I reply, "Let's stay. We should park the car around back near the employee entrance of the hotel. I need time to think of a plan. We know where they are, but not for how long. Lydia's smart. She knows what kind of car you drive and she won't stay in the same place for long. So we have to keep an eye on their hotel from ours." I pause to think of a good vantage point. "We could have a good view from the gym. I could see the entrance to their hotel from the gym windows."

"Awesome! Are you ready for this?"

"As ready as I'll ever be."

CHAPTER 17

Alex decides to wait in our hotel's lobby close to the window so he can see when the girls pull back into the parking lot next door. I need a moment to gather myself, so I head back up to my room to clear my head.

My mind flashes back to when Lydia brought me to the apartment that Sam and I shared so I could grab my things after I was released from the hospital. Each ding of the elevator makes me more and more anxious. I have to brace myself against the elevator's wall to keep from collapsing.

A short time later the doors slide open and I walk down the long corridor to my room. The satisfying slide of the keycard allows me access to a tidy, air-conditioned room with the curtains tightly closed. I flip the light switch and head to the bathroom to wash my face.

Breathe, Leo.

I stare at my reflection in the mirror above the sink for a solid couple of minutes, unrecognizing the man staring back at me. Just a few months ago, my face was cleanly shaven and my cheeks fuller and filled with color. Now I have a full beard that's a little more untamed than I usually like and my face is skinnier. I run my fingers through my beard and decide it's time for a trim.

Luckily, I bought a cheap set of trimmers when we stopped for some new clothes and supplies on the drive out here. I take off my shirt and take a good look at my body. Like my face, it's also skinnier, but still lean. I can make out a full six pack of abs now and I have a slight v-line shape leading to my groin area- all of which has more hair than I'm used to.

I turn on the trimmers and go to town cleaning up my beard just enough to still have one, but a beard that's also edged and short. I make my way down from my beard to my chest and trim the hair until I'm smooth again.

Looking around at the mess of hairs strewn across the bathroom counter, I sweep them with my hand into the sink and rinse them down the drain. I look back at the mirror at a fresh face and clean landscape and I smile. I look great for someone who's been through hell.

My phone rings from my back pocket and I see it's Alex calling me from downstairs.

"Hey," I say, "Are they back?"

"Yeah, they just pulled back in with takeout." Alex replies.

"Oh good. At least she's feeding her."

"It's a little deeper than that, I think, Leo."

Confused, I ask, "What do you mean?"

"They're talking and laughing with each other. It's making me think of some type of Stockholm shit is going on."

I make my way to the bed and sit down at the foot of it. Arie was kidnapped by Lydia. Why would she be laughing with her captor?

"That doesn't make sense," I say.

"I agree. Whatever the reason, I'm sure we'll figure it out soon enough."

"Alright. I'm finishing up here. I'll be down in a minute." I end the call and sit in disbelief for a few seconds before grabbing a black tee shirt from the dresser drawer and my keycard from the bathroom counter. I turn off the light switch and leave my room to head towards the elevators.

When the doors slide open on the lobby level, I can see Alex sitting in a chair near the window. He looks up from his phone, sees me, and stands up to meet me as I walk towards the doors. Once we're outside, we start walking with a quickened pace towards the hotel next door.

"Did you have time to think of a plan?" His eyes wander to my beard. "Looks good, man. I need a shave myself." He runs his hand across his barely-there stubble.

"I think we need to do a little bit of scouting the building first. We know about the front exit, but I think we need to make sure all doors are covered just in case."

Nodding his head, Alex says, "Right. I'll go around the right side of the building and meet you around back by the service doors."

"How do you know there's service doors?"

"Our hotel has them, so I'm assuming this one does, too." He makes a good point.

"Okay. I'll go around the left side of the building and I'll meet you."

We break apart and go about the plan. I try to stay as close to the building as possible and avoid looking up at any windows in case Lydia is looking out for us. Passing the lobby doors, I look inside and see no sign of the girls in the bustling lobby. I do, however, take note of a pretty, blonde girl behind the counter, probably in her early twenties.

That could come in handy, I think.

I round the corner of the building a few yards later and take a mental note of the fire exit as I pass it. I read, "Emergency Exit Only: Alarm Will Sound" and I smile a devilish grin.

Lydia won't be stupid enough to cause a commotion

trying to flee again. Not with all these people around. She's smarter than that. I round the back left corner of the building and see Alex standing near the service doors that the employees use to get in and out of the building for their shifts.

"How many exits did you see?" He says, louder than I would've liked.

"Keep your voice down, dumb ass!" I hiss. "Do you want them to run out the front before we have a chance to cut them off?"

Alex puts his hand up to his mouth and his eyes go wide, "Shit! Sorry, man." He lowers his voice, "How many exits did you see?"

Rolling my eyes, I say, "Only one other than this one and the front. If they're gonna run again, I doubt it'll be out the side exit- it's emergency only. Lydia wouldn't be dumb enough to cause a commotion. I say our best bet is to go in from here and the front. I'll go through the service doors. I need you to go in through the front."

"Dude, I'm no good under pressure. What if I see them? What do I-"

"There's a cute girl working the front desk. Just try to flirt some information out of her. Make something up like you're visiting friends or some bullshit. I need to know what room they're in."

All of a sudden, his expression changes and his face

looks a little more relaxed. "You said she's cute, huh?" He thinks about it for a second, "Okay, I'm game. What are you gonna do, though? What happens if someone sees you?"

"I'll figure that out. Just head around to the lobby. Text me when you find out the room number."

Alex nods and heads back around the building. He brought up a good question: What am I gonna do? I can play this a couple of different ways- I can try to go unnoticed, which I'm sure is only wishful thinking or I can pretend it's my first day of work.

Come on, Leo. Think. Which plan is more doable?

As I'm thinking, a twiggy-looking guy, about sixteen or so walks past and stops to look at me, "Are you new?"

"Me?" I say.

"Yes, you. Who else?" He chuckles as he looks around at no one else.

Guess I'm going with the employee plan. "Oh, yeah. Sorry- first day jitters."

"There's nothing to be nervous about." He says with a wave of his hands. "Want me to show you around?"

"I'd love that." I say, trying too hard to sound nervous for my "first day of work." Get it together.

"Okay, right this way. I have to go to my locker anyway." He says as he holds the door open for me.

We walk into the service hallway and make a right

down another hallway towards what I'm assuming is the employee locker room.

"So what did they hire you for?" He asks, trying to make small talk. He's being friendly, but I can't get sucked into this.

"I'm the new handyman, I guess." I reply without thinking it through.

"Oh, thank God! We need more hands around here," He exclaims as we push open the door to the locker area. "This is where you can put all of your things. Lockers are first come, first served and you have to bring your own locks. The company doesn't supply them."

"That's shitty," I spit out.

"Yeah, but what can we do?" He shrugs his shoulders and takes his backpack off. "Anyway, I'm Chris." He holds his hand out for me to shake.

I reach out to shake his hand, "I'm Leo."

"Nice to meet you, Leo," He says, still with a hint of uncertainty lingering in his voice.

"Thanks, man! You, too." A ding from my phone grabs my attention and I look down to see a text from Alex that reads, "213." That was fast.

"Hey, I have to go. Thank you so much for showing me around."

"So soon?"

Thinking fast, I respond with, "Yeah- boss just texted me. I have a job in 213."

"Oh okay! Be careful- the girls that checked into that room will eat you alive, dude! Bunch of lady killers for sure!"

I let out a light laugh. If only you knew, Chris. If only you knew.

I take the service elevator to the second floor and see a sign pointing right for "Rooms 201-215" and I start in that direction. The hallway feels like it's growing longer and longer as I pass each room. 205. 209. 212. I finally reach room 213 and I freeze. My legs physically will not carry me anymore and I stand in the middle of the hallway, right outside their door. It isn't long before I hear them inside-Lydia and Arie talking to each other like one didn't just kidnap the other.

The fire inside me reignites and my legs start working fine. I feel the urge to absolutely explode but I remain calm, take a few breaths, and knock on their door. I hear the both of them fall completely silent and footsteps come towards the door. I'm staring hard at the peephole and I'm sure that I'm making eye contact with one of them, even though I can't see their face on the other side.

There's a hesitation before the locks are undone. I feel it in my bones and it gives me goosebumps- the utter terror that runs through the body when you know someone has found you in a seemingly winnable game of hide and seek. The locks finish unlatching and the door creaks open.

"Leo." The disappointment in her voice is enough to tear my heart in two. I stare back at Arie's cold expression and all the confidence I once had dissipates in an instant. Looking into her unimpressed eyes, I feel confused and slightly hurt that she wasn't more excited to see me. After all this time, it's like Arie didn't want to be found.

"Arie, I came to take you home," I say, trying to break past whatever wall she had built since she's been gone.

"To the home you burned down? That home?" Her words sting, but I deserved that. I burned down the place that housed the terrible memories of past and present lives. "I don't need saving, Leo. I'm ready to live my life. Sam's dead. You made sure of that. You ended it for all of us."

"No, Arie. It's Lydia, she's-"

"Oh my god. You're impossible."

Shocked, I try to find my words, "Why are you saying all this to me?"

"Because I'm finally free of you." Arie's words will echo forever in my head. "Lydia saved me from that place and from you."

"You don't know what you're saying, Arie. You're suffering from Stock-"

"Stockholm syndrome? Really? A woman makes her

own decisions and all of a sudden she's fucking hypnotized. Men are such misogynistic pieces of-"

"Okay, Arie. That's enough." A third voice chimes in as Lydia walks towards the door out of the shadows of their dimly lit room.

I feel nothing when I see her. I was so angry and hurt by her that I was sure I'd lunge at her throat the first chance I got, but now all I want to do is fall into my bed and never wake up.

"Hello, Leo," she says. "You came all this way to find us? How sweet." She gestures to Arie, who walks away and sits at the desk, staring at the blank wall.

My voice shakes, but I manage to mutter, "What did you do to her?"

"What did I do? Oh, Leo. It's not what I did to Arie. It's what you did and have always done to her. You always have to be the center of the universe and for what?"

"That's not-"

She pushes me up against the wall outside of her hotel room door, pinning me with her forearm. "Listen to me. If you come here again, I'll kill her. Do you understand me, Leo? I will end her fucking life. And then I'll kill Alex in front of you."

"Why are you doing this, Lydia?" Her forearm presses harder, making it more difficult for me to breathe. "What did I do to you?"

Her expression goes blank and the pressure on my neck lessens as she takes a step back, releasing her weight. "You really don't remember, do you?"

"Remember what?" I ask, rubbing my neck while staring at her questioningly.

"Your family took everything from me; my home, my life, and my hope." Tears well in her eyes and for a fraction of a second I feel bad for her, but I still don't know what she's talking about.

"Lydia, from the bottom of my heart, I'm sorry. If I could change everything, I would. Believe me. I need you to believe me." I drop to my knees and look up at her.

Wiping the tears from her eyes, she straightens her posture and exhales deeply. "It's too late for that, Leo. What's done is done. And what's to come is going to be so much worse for you than you can even imagine. Mark my words, Leo- you will know suffering."

She walks past me and shuts the door forcefully. On the other side, I hear the sound of all the locks being bolstered. Instead of moving from the pitiful position I'm in on my knees in the hallway of the hotel, I sink deeper into the ground and shed tears like an endless river of saltiness and suffering.

I need answers. What did I do? What is Lydia going to do? All roads point back to the past. The most important question is: do I have the strength to go searching for the pieces of the puzzle I'm missing?

My phone vibrates and I pull it out of my back pocket to see a text from my dimwitted brother.

"How's it going?" His texts reads.

Somehow, I find strength in his text and pull myself to my feet. I make my way towards the service elevator and press the button for the ground floor. It doesn't take long before the doors slide open and I make my way to the exit I entered through.

Once I'm outside, I start walking back to the hotel where my belongings are and respond to my brother, "We need to talk." The swoosh sound of the text being sent provides me a little bit of comfort and I put the phone back in my pocket.

Tonight, I feel defeated. Tomorrow is a new day.

CHAPTER 18

"She said what?" Alex seems just as confused as I am when it comes to the whole situation. I've gone over the exchange with him twice now and it seems more bizarre the more we talk about it.

Nodding my head, I say, "Listen, the whole thing is fucked up, but the strangest part about it all is that Arie wanted nothing to do with me. She didn't seem like herself."

"I'm telling you, Leo, she's brainwashed. She has Stockholm syndrome and-"

"Enough, Alex. It's more than that. She doesn't have Stockholm syndrome. She literally wasn't being herself. She seemed like a ghost if anything." I can't help but to think of the blank stare Arie had when I was questioning her. "What if she was hypnotized or something?"

Alex looks a bit in shock and remains silent for a few minutes, "Leo, there's a bit more to our story than what you think."

"Oh? Then feel free to enlighten me, Alex. Because right now, I'm scrambling for answers." Hurt, I sit on the edge of the bed. "And it feels like the only person who can give them to me is more inclined to kill me than talk to me."

He sits in the desk chair adjacent to my bed and lets out a deep breath, "Okay. So, here's the thing, bro: Lydia was adopted. That much you know."

"Right. So what am I missing?"

"The Greene's- my parents- took her in to try and give her a new start. They tried to give her a life again. However, Lydia started acting very strange not long after she started living with us. Chickens started going missing, kind of like how they started going missing with Benjamin years later.

So, anyways, my parents confronted her about it and she denied the whole thing, even though they had witnessed for themselves her disappearing into the barn late at night. My mother even claimed to have spotted her cutting the throat of one of the hens and burning the carcass while chanting in some weird, Devil-tongue."

"This sounds like the plot of *The Crucible*, dude."

Rolling his eyes, Alex continues, "Yeah, but this is real. After denying it, my father decided he had had enough of her lies and tried desperately to get her out of the house. That's when he bumped into your adoptive parents and offered her services in exchange for nothing. It wasn't too long before they had adopted you, so they made the offer even more tempting. I still remember them using both of your adoptions as a way of connecting the two of you together."

"Okay, but Alex, what does that have to do with everything? So we were adopted. Big fucking deal. What's the catch?" Impatient, I can't help but to want my brother to get to the point.

"The catch, Leo, is that your family's property used to belong to Lydia's biological family. When the news came to Lydia that she would be shipped to your home to work until a dowry was raised for her to be courted off to some random man, she couldn't have been happier. That was the first time I had even seen her smile since her adoption."

Almost too stunned to speak, I realize that so many things finally made sense. It's the house. The fucking house is the reason for all of this revenge. She was mad at my family.

"That's not it though, Leo." Alex interrupts the thoughts pouring into my mind. "Now that I think about it, the goal was never the house. I think the whole time the goal was to get to the Williams Family."

"What are you saying?" I ask, skeptical of where the story was headed.

"I'm saying I think the whole thing starts before you were adopted by them." He says with a puzzling look on his face. "Do you remember anything from your old childhood that could help answer any of our questions?"

My mind flashes to an orphanage but stops short of any answers I'm searching for. Shaking my head, "Nothing. I don't remember anything before Lydia getting fired that day."

I start thinking of the day she got fired and how she didn't even try to convince my parents to stay. Was that her goal all along? Did she get what she came for? What reasons would she have for quietly disappearing into the night, only to send someone to kill all of us?

Alex continues, "Then I think the best course of action would be to try and get you to remember your childhood, bro. Something has to be in that dense head of yours. Maybe get some rest or meditate or some shit." He stands and pushes the chair under the built-in desk against the wall. "In the meantime, I have a date with that pretty young thing from downstairs." He chuckles and brushes his shoulders off.

"You're too much, Alex," I say, rolling my eyes. "I'll try to look deep and let you know if I can think of anything."

I walk my brother to the door of my hotel room and

grab the door handle. When I open it, Adam is standing outside with his fist up, ready to start knocking.

"Oh, sorry, Leo, I didn't realize you had company. I'll come back-" He starts, cheeks beginning to blush.

"No- you can stay! My brother was just leaving, actually!" I say, turning to look at my brother with an expression of "get the fuck out."

Chuckling, my brother walks through the threshold, switching places with Adam, who's now standing at my side in my room. He says, "Bag it up, boys!" And I slam the door in his face, his laughing continues down the hall towards the elevators.

"I'm so sorry about him," I say, blushing myself now. "What's up?"

"Don't worry about it! And not much- I just can't stop thinking of last night. I feel awful for just leaving, but I had to get home."

Great. He probably has a wife or a husband or something, I think to myself.

"Oh, you're good," The disappointment shows clearly on my face.

"No- I'm not. I've never done anything like that before. I feel awful about leaving without saying goodbye."

"Listen, dude- I already said you're good. I appreciate you stopping by, but I've had hookups before. We're both consenting adults. Just take the win and move on." Cold, but that's how you have to be sometimes.

"Leo, you don't-" He starts. God this gorgeous idiot doesn't get it.

"No, you don't get it. We hooked up. I've been picked up just to be thrown back down again. Stop spreading salt in the wound."

"I'm trying to say I want to take you out."

I fall completely silent and I'm in awe. Am I the idiot? What did he just say?

"Like on a proper date," He continues, the words start streaming out of his gorgeous lips like a refreshing waterfall. "You see, I don't normally hop into bed with someone, but something about you felt different and I wanted you. I still want you, but the right way. Is that crazy?"

"So you're not married?" I ask the only question that comes to mind in the moment.

He starts laughing and grabs my face in his strong, tanned hands. "I haven't been in a relationship in like three years, actually. So I, too, am single as fuck!"

I pull him closer and kiss him deeply, his soft lips overtaking mine easily. He smells like sandalwood and I want him to take me all over again just like he did more than once last night. I start to unbutton his suit jacket, but his hands meet mine at his top button and he stops me in the process.

"Trust me when I say that I want nothing more than another night like last night," he says behind closed eyelids and a clenched, Herculean jaw, "But what I want more is to take you somewhere nice and get to know you better."

Melting with his words, I nod my head and kiss him again, only this time I pull away when he gets a little too into it and it feels good when he gives me that smirk that says, "I want you" while holding both of my hips with a firm grip.

"So can you stay tonight?" I ask, nuzzling his nose with mine, teasing him some more.

He breathes in deeply and holds it for a little while, clearly contemplating on giving me the answer I'm looking for, before letting it out and whispering, "As much as I want to say yes, I start my shift in about ten minutes."

"Fine," I say, acting spoiled. "Then what did you have in mind for our date?"

Shaking his finger in front of my face, "Nope. It's a surprise. Telling you would ruin half the fun of it. Just don't go to sleep yet, okay?"

"Is the date tonight? I thought you were about to start working!"

"I am, but I'm also the manager. If I want to take longer than an hour for my break, then guess what? I'll take longer than an hour for my break. Simple as that." He chuckles and I catch another glimpse of his perfect smile.

"Okay, big shot. I'll try to stay awake for you." I wink at him and his face lights up as he leans in to kiss me again.

"Just text me, okay?" He asks, looking over at the note I put on the bed that he left this morning. "You know, since you haven't yet." His sarcasm is just about as sexy as he is.

He starts walking towards the door and stops when he grabs the handle. Turning one more time to look at me and smile, he turns the knob and exits my hotel room. It doesn't take long for the sadness to creep back into the room as soon as Adam leaves. Today was rough, that's for sure. I don't want to think of another relationship right now, but Adam is making that hard for me. He's making it all hard- even me.

Memories of last night flood my brain and I can't stop myself from sticking my hand down my pants. I pull out my phone to text him, but instead I log on to the hotel's wifi and search Pornhub for whatever's trending. I pull my pants down to my ankles and stare at myself in the full-length mirror across from the bathroom door.

I begin stroking my dick to the sound of hot guys moaning on my phone and my heart starts beating faster and faster. Thoughts of looking down and seeing Adam on his knees looking back up at me with a mouthful of my cock pushes me closer and closer to the edge until I erupt- weaker than I did multiple times last night, but still, something is better than nothing.

I waddle to the bathroom to grab some tissues to clean up the mess I had just made and turn on the shower while I'm next to it. It only takes a minute or two to clean up and I take my clothes the rest of the way off and slip into the warm stream of the hotel shower. As I let it rain down on my closed eyelids, an overwhelming sense of dread comes over me. Not because I had just jerked off to a mixture of cheap porn and the thought of a demigod-like hotel manager, but because I remembered the shitty day I had just been dealt.

My best friend hates me and I'm left with more questions than answers. To top it all off, the guy I hooked up with, gorgeous as he may be and as sweet as he's proving to be so far, came into my life at the absolute wrong time.

Such is my life, I suppose.

After my shower, I bring my phone out again and type his number from the note he left me in the new, blank message box staring back at me. I type, "Hey, you! It's Leo," and hesitate before sending.

Is that too basic? Should I send more? At this point, does it even matter? The familiar swooshing sound of the message being sent brings me a moment of giddy bliss again before the reality of my life catches me off guard.

Still holding my phone, I search my recent call log and tap on Alex's name. It rings a few times before it's obviously ignored and I get his voicemail.

"Alex, it's Leo. We need to go over a plan. I need answers," I say, unsure of exactly how to go about getting them.

Once I end the call, I sit at the edge of my bed, looking around the empty, dimly lit hotel room and ponder the idea of potentially starting a relationship with Adam. I go over an all but too quick list of pros versus cons and decide right now isn't the best time. Disappointed, I lay back in bed and stare at the ceiling. My eyelids grow heavier as I feel my eyes start to well up with tears.

I pay attention to the sound of the air conditioning blowing through the vent and feeling of the tears gliding down the sides of my face, tickling the small hairs of my sideburns on their way to the sheets. I close my eyes completely and fall asleep as commonly as I do these days-sad and disappointed with myself.

CHAPTER 19

"Evan, my dear," I'm woken from my sleep by the head mistress of the orphanage I currently reside in. A kind, caring woman, she also knows no boundaries. For instance, when someone is sleeping, you let them be.

"Yes, Mother Donna?" I say, groggily. After tossing and turning for most of the night, I had only just recently fallen into a deep sleep.

"It's adoption day, my child. Your new family is waiting for you downstairs," She says quietly as to not disturb the other boys in the room. "And they're excited to finally take you home."

I sit up in bed quickly, suddenly not phased by the lack of sleep I was having. I finally get to leave this place and start a life and the excitement hits me like a wagon of bricks.

"Now get dressed and we'll meet you downstairs in a few moments." The door closes softly behind her and I hear her muffled footsteps waddle away.

Mother Donna has been the only form of guardianship I've known. Her and the other nuns that run Cumberland Boys Home have played a huge roll in the way I grew up seeing as I've been in the orphanage since I was only but a few days old. The Sisters and Mother Donna found me late one night with a note asking them to take care of me. At least that's the story I've been told.

I believe a different story altogether- especially since the Sisters exaggerate a different part of the story each time it's told. I'm old enough now to know when someone is lying to me and one day I'll find out. Maybe not today or tomorrow, but one day I will learn the truth about my biological family.

I finish getting dressed and stuffing the few items I own into my jacket pockets- small trinkets I've acquired on the playground over the years. A penny from two years ago that has all but lost its shine; a piece of ribbon I believe to have belonged to a beautiful girl; and a rock with a flashing of fire depending on how the light hits it. These are my possessions and while they may not make sense to the other Sisters, Mother Donna tells me to hold my belongings close. My possessions don't define me, rather they tell a small part of my story. Behind each of them is a piece of my memories. These are the first things I've ever owned.

Today, however, my collections grow- I now have a family. More specifically, I have a mother and father. I've never met them, but I've seen them upon their entry to the orphanage. He, a tall, fair-skinned man with graying hair, dressed to the nine, and her, a slender, brown-haired woman with the widest smile I've ever seen. Plus, the carriage they rode in on was something out of a fairytale- extremely ornate with a couple of prize show-horses pulling it behind them.

My life is getting ready to start a new chapter and I've never been more excited. As I make my way to the bedroom door, I stop to turn around and look at the bed I called mine these last however many years. Before today, I was just another boy sleeping in another bed with a thin blanket. Now, I'll be the boy that gets his own room. I'll be the boy that gets a mother and a father and learns to read and write like proper children do.

Tomorrow, I'll be a man with a wife of my own and a son like me- only I'll be there for him. I'll never leave him alone like my parents did to me. He'll know love and he'll be able to pass that to his children as well.

I promise I won't be like them, I think to myself. I'll be better. I promise.

I enter Mother Donna's office where my new parents are facing away from me. They must have heard me come in, because they readjusted themselves in their chairs before turning to look at me.

"You must be Evan," The woman starts. "Hello, child. My name is Olivia. This is my husband, Thomas."

Her eyes are kind and welcoming. “We’re bringing you home today- Son.” When she calls me Son, my soul fills with hope and love immediately and I don’t know how to respond with anything but tears.

“Mother, Father!” I say as I race across the room into her open arms. Still unsure of what came over me, I linger there and can feel Mr. Williams’s hand rubbing my back in a circular motion. “Thank you! Thank you!”

“Come, Son,” Mr. Williams says. “It’s time we get you to your new home.”

After saying my goodbyes to Mother Donna and the rest of the Sisters standing on the front stoop, I step into the carriage with the help of my adoptive father and take a seat on a violet-colored velvet seat. The color makes me want to vomit, but the seat itself is one of the most comfortable things I’ve ever felt.

“Ready to see your new house?” Mrs. Williams asks. I nod my head in her direction and begin watching the foliage outside the carriage move behind us as we make our way to my new home. “We’ve recently renovated the home, you see, so in a way, this is something new for all of us that we can share together.”

“Indeed, that was wonderfully put, my dear,” Mr. Williams responds.

I’m not sure what came over me in Mother Donna’s office when I called two perfect strangers mother and father, but now it doesn’t feel as natural. I’d like to think that calling them mother and father will get easier, but as for right now, Mr. and Mrs. Williams will have to do.

"This is all so very exciting. Thank you again. I promise I won't let you down." I say, way more depressing than I wanted to sound. "It's just- I haven't ever had a home before, so I'm a bit nervous and excited at the same time. I want this to work."

"Well you're in luck, Son. We've never done this either, so I guess we just have to help each other along the way," Thomas says optimistically.

When we finally arrive at the house, I'm more inclined to call it a manor or an estate. It's a beast of a house and it sits by itself in the middle of a clearing with a long road leading up to it. There's an iron and stone gate at the front and it seems like it's covered in some type of vine I can't make out from this distance.

As we pull up to the giant front door of my new home, I feel peace settling in for the first time in a long time. I finally have a family and a home. What child wouldn't feel peaceful?

The front door opens as I step out of the carriage and there's a blonde girl standing in the doorway waving. She isn't much older than I am, based off her appearance- maybe twelve or thirteen years old- and she's in worker's clothes so I'm assuming she's a housekeeper of some kind.

"Evan, this is Lydia," My new mother says. "She helps out around the house as needed."

"Welcome home, Mr. and Mrs. Williams.," Lydia says to my parents and then turns her attention towards me. "And welcome home to you as well, Evan. I'm Lydia. Nice to make your acquaintance." She curtsies and moves towards the carriage to unpack it before it gets parked near the barn off to the side of the manor.

Walking through the gigantic door, I'm reminded of a certain privilege that some people have versus others. If you had asked me a week ago where I thought I was going to end up, I wouldn't have ever imagined being in a house such as this. The foyer is a marvelous two stories with decorative wooden spindles going up the stairway like a spine. The details are impressive to say the least- right down to the ornate oriental rug in the center of the room, being bolstered to the floor by a solid, hand-carved table.

This is just the first room, I think to myself. There's a whole house beyond this one!

"Why don't you settle in, Son?" My new father asks. "There are three empty rooms upstairs. The first one on the right as soon as you get to the top of the staircase is your mother's and mine, so feel free to choose any of the remaining three for yourself!"

Excitedly, I hurry up the stairs, barely grabbing onto the railing on my way to the top. Once I'm at the landing, I look out over the railing and see the cord holding the chandelier seemingly just out of reach and the height of the room suddenly makes me nervous. I back away from the edge and turn around to face the hallway. On my right is my parents' bedroom door. Across from them is another room. I continue walking down the hallway and notice a door on my right and a little further down the hall is two more doors across from each other. I open the one on the right and take note of a bathroom complete with a sink, toilet, and beautiful clawfoot tub. The room is immaculately cleaned. Everything has a slight sparkle to it and it makes me feel relieved to not have to share with thirty other boys anymore.

Closing the door behind me, I cross the hall and grab the door handle to the last bedroom on the left. When I open it, there's a slight creaking sound coming from the hinges and I enter a spacious, airy room. Complete with an armoire, dresser, and bed, I barely notice the giant mirror leaning against the wall.

Deciding this room will be mine, I leap into bed and lay there for a while, just taking comfort in the soft mattress and sheets. This bed is a tremendous upgrade from the one at the orphanage- there's not one spring jumping out at a moment's notice to poke my backside. I sit up in bed and startle myself slightly when I meet my own gaze in the mirror against the wall.

Climbing out of the giant bed, I get closer to my reflection and see something that I had not noticed before now- happiness. I can see it in my eyes. My skin seems to be glowing, my frown has disappeared, and my eyes seem content for the first time in a long time, if ever.

I hear the creak of the door behind me and notice in the reflection Lydia poking her head around the door, "Evan, your mother and father sent me to fetch you for lunch. They'd like to eat in the gardens this afternoon."

"Okay, thank you. I'll be down in a bit." I say, still in awe of such a rich thing being said to me. Eating lunch in the gardens.

The door to my room closes and I let out a silenced shriek of excitement. This is it. This is finally living.

CHAPTER 20

Walking through the front door of my new home, I exit onto the front porch. I look out over the yard as I close my eyes and take in the scent of the warm breeze. It's sweet like honey with a hint of cedar from the trees surrounding the property. My curious nose leads me back to the gate I had only recently come through on my journey to this place and I'm excited to find that the vine I had noticed from inside the carriage is in fact wild honeysuckle.

I pull a flower from the vine and give the green bulb a pinch as I pull it from the pedals with a small drop of the sweet nectar I've only tasted a small handful of times before. I close my eyes again as the blissful feeling overcomes me for the hundredth time since I first opened my eyes this morning.

"What are you doing?" Lydia chuckles as she approaches from behind me.

I spin around like I had just been caught by one of the sisters for doing the same thing on the playground of the boys' home, "It's honeysuckle."

"Honeysuckle? What's that?"

I point towards the vine growing heavily along the gate, "These little white flowers. Each one has a single drop of honey in them."

"Are you lying?" She says, curious grin on her face.

"Watch- I'll show you!" I pull two flowers from the vine and pass one to Lydia. "Do like me," I say, continuing to mutilate the flower to retrieve the nectar from within.

I taste my reward as I watch Lydia's expression go from that of confusion to one of excitement, "Impossible!" She exclaims, "How did you know that?"

"One of the sisters showed me at the orphanage I lived at. It's a quick way to have a sweet treat on warm summer days like this."

"Incredible!" She says, pulling another flower for herself.

Behind her, my mother waves me over from the small bistro set in the gardens across the yard.

"I have to go to lunch. Will you join us?" I ask my new friend timidly.

"I'd love to!"

We race each other to where my new parents are sitting in the garden, waiting for lunch. Our laughter echoes across the spacious grounds and as we near my adopters, I notice their expressions dim and smiles fade. With the disappearance of their happiness, our running also deduces to a steady walk.

I clear my throat and look at Mrs. Williams first. She seems the kinder of the two, so I ask, "Mother, may Lydia join us for lunch in the garden?"

"Lydia has chores to tend to, Son." Mr. Williams answers before his wife has a chance to open her mouth. "Besides, this is a family meal. We have lots to talk about."

Lydia stiffens her posture and straightens her apron, "Of course, Mr. Williams. I'll get started on those chores right away. If there's anything I can gather for you three, please don't hesitate to ask."

With a final curtsey before she exits the patio, Lydia bows her head and looks at me expressionless before meandering back towards the house. When she's far enough away, I notice her shoulders slouch and I can only imagine she's hurt by Thomas's words.

"That certainly could have been handled more nicely, Thomas," Mrs. Williams says curtly. "The poor girl was basically pawned off on us and you treat her as if she's just the help."

"She is the help, Olivia. We pay her to do the chores. What good is she if she can't finish even the simplest of tasks?"

"Dear God above, Thomas. Where's your humanity?"

"Olivia- enough. We'll speak on this later," He waves his hands at her as to shush her and his gaze turns towards me. "Now, Evan, there's a lot to discuss. The Williams Family is a very respected family in New York. My father inherited a large amount of land from his father. With that land, he built a community. Eventually the community blossomed with businesses and banks. Our family still owns a fair share of the properties on our old land, but have pulled back from city life to move to the countryside where you stand this very moment," My eyes grow wide in amazement as I realize he's talking about this property. "One day, I'd like to see you become the next Williams man to take over for me like I did for my father."

"So your father built this house after moving to the countryside?" I ask, completely disregarding the main point of his story.

"Not quite, Son. You see, there used to be a small house stationed on the same spot our home is currently located. My father passed away before this house could be built. I inherited the property and started the build. What was there before was an awful mess of rotting wood and dirt floors. It smelled of death and mildew and the family that used to own it eventually came around to our offer to purchase the land from them. As you can see, the small, decrepit house that once was is no longer so. Instead, our beautiful manor sits proudly upon the rubble of that hut."

"That's an incredible story, Mr. Williams," I say, trying to sound polite and professional. "Thank you for sharing."

Olivia sits up in her chair, "Enough chatting about the past- our food is growing cold."

We each enjoy a wonderful meal together- the first of many, I hope. I start off eating quickly, like I've never once had a lunch in my life. Realizing how inappropriately I was behaving, I make eye contact with Thomas- whose stare is boring a hole through my head- and slow down to a steady pace with careful, slow chews. It takes everything I have not to shovel the entire plate down my gob in one strong swooping motion.

Once I start eating with the correct etiquette, I glance over at Olivia, who nods in my direction with a smile on her face. Her expression tells me that she can see I'm trying. I want this to work. I need this to work. All I've ever known is the orphanage and I cannot go back.

"I never got the chance to really thank the both of you for adopting me," I start after wiping the corners of my mouth with my linen napkin. "I can't tell you how much it means to me to have a home finally. I thought for sure I'd age out of the orphanage and have to go to work in a stable somewhere just to survive."

Mr. and Mrs. Williams trade looks with each other before they both turn towards me.

"Son, you don't need to thank us. We wanted a son as much as you wanted a home, I'm sure. So in a way, we both have helped each other," Thomas starts talking again, before Olivia has the chance for a second time. "Please- don't thank us. And may I ask a favor?"

"Absolutely, Mr. Williams. Anything."

"Call me Father?"

My heart palpitates suddenly and I'm left speechless. I've never said the word "Father" out loud and actually meant it- aside from earlier this morning when I blurted it out. I've never had an actual father to call for, so it takes me by surprise when the first favor I'm asked to perform is one of great meaning.

I ask myself, what is a father? This is probably as good as it gets, Evan. It's a simple word. You know how to say it, so just spill it. Call him father. Call. Him. Father.

I look over at Olivia, who's sitting opposite Thomas and is in just about as much shock as I am. Turning back toward Thomas, I reply, "Anything for you, Father. And for you, Mother."

I can tell this moment means a great deal to the both of them and I feel the same way. I've never called someone mother or father and actually felt like the words carried any meaning. The looks on their faces are of such pure affection that I could melt.

We finish our meals and sit silently, but full of joy. On our walk back to the house, Lydia walks past us to clean up the meal we all just shared in the garden. I try to smile in her direction, but she keeps her eyes forward, unaware of my attempt to get her attention. As I grow nearer and nearer to the manor doors, I stop to look back at her and see her shoulders slouched again as she gathers the dishes my parents told me to leave where they were on the table.

Every muscle in my body is urging me to go and help clean up, but my father seemingly notices my hesitation and ushers me through the door into the house. I have to pretend like it doesn't bother me- at least for the time being. I need this life more than anything. I can't risk jeopardizing it because I break my father's rules.

Later in the evening, my father retired to the parlor and sat quietly in front of the fireplace, glass full of some brown liquid in hand. All I know is that the liquid he pours again and again for himself smells sickly sweet like a bottle of thick molasses.

My mother joins him in the parlor and too sits quietly in front of the fire, book in hand. I'd never imagined any mother of mine to be reading so fluently in the company of her husband, but my parents' relationship seems a little more like a mutual understanding or some type of non-verbal agreement that keeps them both content.

Feeling the tiredness setting in, I stretch my arms while sitting silently on the parlor couch, I say softly, "I think I'm going to retire to my chambers, if that's okay."

Mother tilts her head to look over at me, "Of course, child. Goodnight."

"Goodnight, Mother, Father." I turn and run up the stairs before my father has a chance to say it back.

When I arrive at my chamber door, I twist the doorknob and enter my new space. Lighting a few pillar candles, I spread them throughout the room to illuminate the darkness- at least until I'm tired enough again to fall asleep.

Why is it that when I sit stationary on a couch, I can fall asleep to the sound of the wind blowing against the glass, but as soon as I stand up to move to an actual bed, I can't fall asleep as quickly? It drives me mad.

I change into my nightclothes and lay back in bed, feet dangling over the edge. I stare at the ceiling until I finally feel the sleep sinking in. It's creeping for now, but it's getting stronger. Tomorrow, I need to plan the rest of my life.

Tonight, however, I sleep soundly knowing I have a mother and father for the first time in my life.

CHAPTER 21

I wake up in my hotel room the same I have every morning for a week- depressed and unmotivated. Alex tries each morning to get me out of the room to explore the area. He thinks that since we're here, we might as well adventure out on the town and check out the localities. But I don't want to check out the town. I don't want to leave my room or my bed.

What started off as just a couple of nights in the hotel was stretched to a week so far. Adam was kind enough to extend our stay- even though I had to take a rain check on our date- but without getting him in trouble, I know we have to prepare to move to either a different room or a different hotel altogether. The one next door is completely off limits for obvious reasons.

I really like Adam and I want to let him into my life, but now isn't a good time at all. He's such an amazing guy and if I'm going to consider starting anything with him, I need to make sure he's safe. With Lydia in the world, he isn't. None of us are.

I sit up in bed, in the dark of the room that hasn't seen light in days and grab my phone from the side table. The brightness is all the way down, but still brighter than my eyes can adjust to right away. Squinting at the lock screen, I enter my passcode and open my texts. Unread messages dot the screen, but the only one I need right now is Alex.

"Hey Alex, when you get a chance, can you come to my room?" I send the text and stand up to walk to the bathroom to wash my face.

His reply says he'll be over in fifteen minutes, so I figure that's plenty of time to shower. Turning on the water, I make sure it's cooler than usual. I need the stimulation and cool water is also supposed to help your body feel better- or so I've read. I undress and look at myself in the mirror briefly, trying awkwardly not to make eye contact with myself. The beard is growing a little out of control and my skin is a little paler, too- probably due to the lack of sunshine bleeding into my room. I have, after all, had the blackout curtains closed and pinched shut with chip clips, so after living like a vampire for a week, it's no surprise why I'm more pale.

I step into the brisk waterfall of the shower and to my surprise it feels good. It's almost nostalgic of being younger and jumping into a cold pool on a hot day without testing the water by dipping your toes in first. The other kids are cheering your name, thinking you're so brave for jumping into the icy waters before them.

I close my eyes and stand directly under the rainfall, feeling the slight pressure drumming on my closed eyelids. It feels good. The touch, I mean. It's comforting to feel something other than just sex. Water doesn't care what you look like. Water cleanses.

When I'm finished with my shower, I dry off and style my hair. For the first time in a long time, I can almost start to recognize myself again. I make my way back to the bedroom and over to the curtains, unclipping them and flinging them open. The morning sun pours into my room with warmth and brightness and for a second I feel at peace. Only for a second though. A knock on my door startles me and I remember it's Alex coming over as requested.

"One second!" I say, before grabbing some briefs from my dresser drawer and a pair of sweatpants.

Opening the door for him, Alex walks through the

threshold, "Damn, bro. It smells awful in here. Maybe let housekeeping do their thing?"

"Fuck off, dude. It isn't that bad," I say, suddenly second-guessing myself. "Anyway, I wanted you to come over because I had another dream. Only this time Lydia and I were kids."

"Oh okay! So tell me everything you remember." He says, suddenly intrigued. He sits down in the desk chair adjacent to my bed.

After explaining to my brother everything I remember from my dream, I sit there waiting for him to speak.

"That's not a lot of information, to be honest. All you remember is a childhood where you met Lydia. I'm not seeing the importance of two kids meeting," He shrugs his shoulders.

"It's not the fact that two kids met, Alex. It's beyond that. It's the fact that Lydia was always- and I mean, always- regarded as the help. Never as family. Maybe she did all of this out of spite."

"That sounds super petty, bro. You really think she'd do this all over the course of however many lifetimes just because she was treated wrongly?"

Realizing how dumb my suggestion really was, I reply, "I guess not. But I still think it's worth finding more about.

Who knows? Maybe I'll have more dreams and they'll actually give me useful information."

"I'm really curious about the small house though."

"The what?"

"From your dream. The small house that was flattened by the manor your family built on top of it. What's the importance of that place?"

Considering the point Alex just made, I realize I'm also curious about the significance of the smaller, now long-gone house. "I wonder if Lydia knows anything about it."

"Worth a shot."

It took a lot for me to build up the confidence to talk to Lydia. So finally, standing outside her door, I hesitate before knocking. What if she doesn't want to talk? She already threatened to kill Arie. I brush off the thought and reach my fist out to knock anyway. Before my knuckles touch the door, it starts to open.

Lydia stands tall in the doorway, glaring at me, "What?"

"I need to talk to you, Lydia." I manage to say confidently, despite feeling the opposite, "Please."

Closing the door in my face, I watch her roll her eyes. With a split-second decision, I wedge my foot in the threshold of the door, blocking her from slamming it in my face. The door opens far enough for Lydia's frame to fit perfectly in it.

She stares at me silently for a few seconds, before she lets out a sigh, "Fine. Not here. Let's talk in the parking lot. I don't want Arie involved any more than she is."

We walk to the parking lot of her hotel silently. It isn't an awkward silence- just empty. Each ding of the elevator is as familiar a sound as it always has been, but this time the dings echo inside my head, reverberating around my skull until the doors slide open and we enter the lobby. It's only when the lobby doors open and we walk outside into the sunlight that the world doesn't seem so quiet.

Birds are chirping, splashing around in small fountains scattered about the hotel's gardens. The steady sound of the sprinklers humming to life mimics the steady drum of the shower head from this morning. The peaceful sounds of the world are interrupted by Lydia.

"What do you want, Leo?" Lydia says, rolling her eyes.

"I want to know why you're doing this. How are you doing this?"

"I'm not telling you how. Not yet. But why? I think you already know why. Maybe you had a dream about it. Or maybe Alex gave you some information that helped you remember."

"Humor me, then."

"Because your family took everything away from me,

Leo. The house my family owned was burned to the ground with my parents inside. By your grandfather."

"What? No- I just had a dream where I remembered my father telling me a story of our family buying the land from a family and then building the manor on the grounds."

"Bullshit. My family never wanted to sell. They realized the potential of the lands they called home and wouldn't sell. Only after both my parents were murdered for their land was the property eventually sold. And on top of the ashes- the manor was built. Your family's manor. I was too young to inherit the property from my parents' will. If I hadn't been playing in the woods surrounding the property that day, I probably would've been burned alive, too."

"Lydia-"

"I was sent to the orphanage where I sat waiting for six years. Six fucking years, Leo. I watched as so many kids- many of whom were younger than me, by the way- were adopted left and right. In the worst turn of events, I was adopted by an older, awful couple- Mr. and Mrs. Greene. They already had a son, but he wasn't enough. You want to know the most ironic part? I was immediately sent to work for the family that murdered mine and burned our house to the ground to make way for theirs."

"Lydia, I-"

"It was that very day- my first day at that house- that I realized what I had to do. So I got to work. Slowly, but surely I started planning how I was going to rid the world of the family that plagued it. Your family was going to suffer. I wanted them to know pain for what they did to mine. A thousand lifetimes or more they would know suffering. But then you came along."

Shocked, I start, "I came along? What do you mean?"

"The day you were adopted, I was going to kill them. I didn't know how exactly, but I had had enough of them treating me like a slave. I was going to end them. Then you came and you brought with you a warmth. I felt hope. We clicked instantly together and I finally had a friend. You showed me the honeysuckle and finally the world was just as sweet again."

I stand there quietly, thoughts running rampant in my mind, trying to put two and two together.

"Eventually, you made me fall in love with you, Leo. What we shared was real, even if you eventually fell for someone else, it was real. And you, just like your family before you, broke my heart. The only thing I had left in the world was you and you didn't fight hard enough for me when your father wanted to send me back to those awful Greenes."

"What was I supposed to do, Lydia? My father was in charge! I couldn't stop him even if I had wanted to." I protest.

"Oh, but you could. You had way more pull over

him than you care to admit. Your mother did, too." She straightens her blouse. "Regardless, what's done is done and I vowed to take my revenge. So that's exactly what I'm doing, Leo."

Speechless, I stand there staring at her, trying desperately to find any bit of life left in her eyes. She clearly feels emotion still- even if it's anger. I think the biggest thing left to find out is how she's managed to bring us all back again and again.

"If that's all, I'd like to get back to Arie." She says, begrudgingly.

"That's all."

"Okay." She walks away from me and through the hotel doors.

I walk back to my hotel feeling like a child that had just be scolded. I'm at a complete loss for words and even my thoughts seem to have subsided a great deal. All I hear is the sound of an occasional car going by or the hum of the central air conditioning units outside the hotel roaring to life sporadically.

This much is clear- I have to find out how she's doing this. And how to stop her.

CHAPTER 22

Later that night, after my chat with Lydia, I pace around my room, trying desperately to build up scenarios of how to deal with her, just to tear my own ideas down. I want answers. How is she doing this to us? Is it some type of magic? Voodoo? Are the stars aligning?

Considering the idea of some type of supernatural phenomena seems to be the easiest way to help explain what's going on, but I can't come up with a solid explanation. What Lydia is doing to us seems to be biblical- with the reincarnation and all, but nothing about what she's doing seems to be under the word of God.

No- there's something more evil at play here. Lydia has to have tapped into some dark shit. Or maybe this is my personal hell and I'm being punished for the mistakes of my father.

My phone starts ringing and I look down to see Arie's name light up my screen. I hesitate before answering, just in case it's Lydia. My heart is beating a million times a minute and my hands immediately start sweating and shaking, but I still manage to swipe my thumb across the touchscreen to answer.

"H-hello?" I stutter.

"Leo?" I let out a sigh of relief and my heart rate slows some when I hear Arie's voice respond to my failed attempt at a confident greeting.

"Arie? Are you okay? We will save you! Just hang in-"

"Leo- stop. I wanted to call and let you know that we're leaving tomorrow morning. Lydia and I are leaving. Please don't follow us. Move on."

"No, Arie! You don't-" I protest, but the line goes dark. She ends the call before I have a chance to convince her otherwise.

I throw my phone onto the bed, feeling defeated, and drop to my knees. The urge to shed some tears comes over me, but my tear ducts are so dried out lately that I just sit there silently instead. I can't think of a good enough reason to call her back, so instead, I start packing my bags.

An anger washes over me that reignites the fire to fight again. It's clear that Arie is definitely brainwashed or under a spell or whatever. She doesn't want us to follow her, but I'll do just that.

I look at the alarm clock on the nightstand next to my bed and see the time read 1:22AM and figure Alex is asleep in his room already. As much as I've loved being on the road with my brother, I feel like he's done his part getting me this far. If I have to face Lydia, I'll do it alone. I don't want anyone else I love coming under her trance or worse- getting killed. She's already taken enough from me. I refuse to let her take anything or anyone else.

I sneak out of my hotel room, with my suitcases packed tightly- a combination of clean and dirty clothes jammed together in harmony. Figuring out which is which will be tomorrow's problem. I walk down the hall silently and press the call button on the elevator. I hear the distance dings of the elevator growing louder as they approach my floor.

Once they slide open, I'm standing face to face with Adam and I can't control my smile. By the looks of it, he can't either until he takes notice of the suitcases behind me and my hoodie draped over my forearm.

"Leaving without a goodbye?" He says, smile fading dreadfully slow.

I want to tell him to come with me. I want to turn

around and walk back to my room with him, but I also want him to be safe. With me- that isn't an option. Instead of saying something sweet or something to show my feelings for him, I drawn in a deep breath and can feel my smile fade away as well.

"Adam, this has been the best few days I've had in a long time all thanks to you."

"But?" He says, hurt in his voice.

"But, I come with a lot of baggage and right now, I don't think it's the best time to start something of a relationship. It was fun, but I need to go."

"Oh, yeah, of course. I just was coming to see if you needed anything. Great. Let's head down and get you checked out, Mr. Daniels." He takes a step back into the elevator and places his arm in front of the sliding doors to hold them open for me.

"Adam, I-"

"I can't hold the doors forever, Mr. Daniels."

I stand for a second, realizing that I had just broken both of our hearts and nod my head. My eyes start to well up with tears and I don't have the courage to make eye contact with Adam. I stand with my back to him and wait impatiently for the doors to open on the ground floor.

As soon as they slide open, seemingly slower than usual, I quicken my pace to the front counter and wait for him to meet me on the other side. He doesn't make eye contact with me either as he continues typing on the hotel's computer, finalizing my check out.

"And you're all set, Mr. Daniels. I do hope you enjoyed your stay with us. In your check out email, you'll find a survey. It would be much appreciated if you'd so kindly provide us your generous feedback. Have a great day!"

I can't think of the words to say to him, so I turn and all but run to the parking lot.

I feel humiliated for Adam. I hate that I had to break things off, but if it means that he'd be safe, then I'd do it again. I wouldn't trade my time with him for anything, either. He has been the only person this past week that has really helped take my mind off the obvious distractions.

As I make my way to the car my brother and I drove here in, I place my belongings in the trunk and then sink into the driver's seat, struggling to find the motivation I only just had a few moments ago. I lean my head on the steering wheel and close my eyes, pinpointing the exact location of an incoming migraine and reach for the glovebox to down some Tylenol.

When the compartment opens, I feel around blindly for the canister of headaches pills and instead feel the cold metal of something solid. My eyelids fling open and I lean over to see the shiny exterior of Alex's Glock he had brought with him for the trip, "for protection," he said, because, "you never know."

Suddenly the motivation finds me again, and I'm left with the disturbing thought of threatening Lydia with it until she tells me the truth. I shake my head and rub my eyes, hoping to wipe away the vivid imagery I have in my head of the very thought.

Only if absolutely necessary, I tell myself.

I reach towards the ignition with key in hand and fire up the car's engine. When it comes to life, I feel the cool breeze of the vents kicking on and then turn off the AC until the car finishes warming up. Thankfully, it doesn't take long and I turn the air back on to warm up the interior.

Deciding that where I'm parked probably isn't the best spot, I drive across the street to the back of a Denny's parking lot and park in a spot with eyes still on the girls' car. I figure I'll wait here as long as I need to be able to follow them when they decide to up and leave. I turn out my headlights and sit patiently.

With the first rays of the morning sun, I realize I had just sat quietly and blankly for about four hours, watching the Navigator I know all too well as if it were just going to drive itself out of the parking and away to freedom. I have to tell myself I'm not crazy a few times before I start to actually believe it.

Realizing I had started to atrophy, I throw open the

driver's side door and step out to stretch. It feels good, opening up my limbs and feeling the slight tear of my muscles as the stretch invigorates my blood vessels.

When I pull the door closed behind me, I look out over the roadway and see the girls walking out of the hotel, bags being rolled behind them on their way to the SUV. I can see Lydia eyeballing the entire parking lot of the hotel I only recently called home for the past week and Arie behind her, staring blankly and emotionlessly ahead.

Lydia uses her key fob to open the trunk of the SUV and gestures at Arie to place all the bags inside. It isn't long before they're both sitting in the front seats and the exhaust is blowing out the white smog you can only see on cooler mornings.

They're finally headed out and I switch the car into drive, ready to follow them to the end of the Earth. When we get to wherever that is, I'm going to make sure I push Lydia over the edge- metaphorically and physically if need be.

CHAPTER 23

After driving for about two hours north, the girls finally pull into the parking lot of an abandoned warehouse and park near the building. I decide it's best not to follow them, so I station my car just outside the entrance to the parking lot, paralleled between a dilapidated pickup truck and an older Mercedes.

I watch as Lydia gets out of the Navigator and walks around to the door. She tries pulling on the door but realizes it's proving pointless to pull on a door that's bolstered with a huge sheet of plywood. She places both hands on her hips in a way that leads me to believe she's frustrated. As if on the drive over she assumed that a vacant warehouse would just be left open.

I roll my eyes hard and feel my phone start vibrating

again. I look down and see Alex's name come across the screen. Swiping across the screen, I ignore the call for the seventh time this morning. Each time, he refuses to leave a voicemail- not surprisingly at all. He's worried and for good reason. I am too.

Finally, the ding of the voicemail notification goes off and I raise my volume loud enough to hear it without putting my phone on speaker.

"Yo, Leo. It's Alex. What the fuck, man? You took my car? You didn't even say you were leaving. I tried your door a couple times before I went downstairs to the lobby to see what was up. According to your boyfriend, you checked out super late last night. That's fucked up, dude. I thought we were in this together and now you stole my car, my gun, and you're ignoring my calls and texts. Call me back, Leo. Please."

I close out of the voicemail app and turn my attention back to the SUV sitting lonely near the entrance to the warehouse. The difference this time is that I can't see Lydia, nor can I see Arie. The plywood looks pried away from the door just enough for people their frame to squeeze through.

Fuck. I pull out of my spot and into the parking lot to get closer now that the coast seems clear. As I approach the car, I decide to park around the side of the warehouse in case they're looking out of some vantage point I've yet to discover.

Once parked, I turn off the car and exit as quietly as I possibly can, even making sure to press the door into the latched position, rather than close it normally. Once the latch clicks into the closed position, the car lets out the forgotten beep sound that newer cars automatically do, no matter how loudly or softly the doors are closed.

I freeze and try to listen for any rustling sounds coming from inside the building in between pulses of my heartbeat which seem louder than usual. It's clear that no one heard the sound and I'm overthinking, but the humility drowns me for a few long seconds, and I start towards the door once the warmth in my cheeks subsides a bit. As I make my way closer to the plywood the girls had pried away slightly from the warehouse entrance, I notice that the gap is big enough for me to fit through now thanks to the depression and lack of appetite I've been experiencing the last few weeks.

I slide through the gap, trying not to get snagged on any screws poking through the side I'm traveling past and feel relief when I make it through unscathed. Inside, the building is barren. There is no furniture, no people, no sound. It almost seems otherworldly. As dystopian as this building seems, Lydia and Arie are definitely here- somewhere.

Just as I start walking towards the back of the building, a sound echoes from the left, coming from the darkness and I can make out the sound of a door opening and closing, followed by a couple of voices coming from where I'm assuming is behind the door. I walk slowly in the direction of the sounds and find myself just outside an old office door with frosted glass.

There's a slight glow coming from inside the door and I can barely make out a few figures standing inside the room. The voices are clearer now, and I can tell one is Lydia, but I'm not sure of the other. It sounds like a man.

Strange, I think to myself. I don't remember seeing another car in the parking lot.

Just as I step away from the door, I turn around to see Arie standing silently behind me, her eyes sunken in the way they do when one doesn't get enough sleep. Her expression is blank and it almost doesn't look like she's looking at me.

"Arie?" I whisper, "Are you okay?" I reach out towards her slowly, trying to place my hand on her shoulder.

In an instant, her eyes flash towards me and her expression bends her face into a frightening grin as she grabs my shoulders and throws me to the ground. On my way down, I glance up at her and notice her eyes are black. I see no whites in her eyes as she leaps on top of me, scratching at my face and screaming a blood-curdling scream.

I manage to grab hold of her hands and shove her off of me to the side with whatever strength I can manage to find. I stand up and start to run when I feel Arie's hands wrap around my ankles and pull my legs out from under me. I fall hard on my stomach and it knocks the air out of my chest. I flip over just in time to see Arie crawling up my legs towards me.

Panic starts to set in as I start flailing my legs, kicking desperately at my aggressor. I manage to kick her off of me and scoot back up against the wall as Arie starts crawling at me again.

"Arie, stop!" I yell at her, now about fifteen feet from me.

The grin never leaves her face as she slowly starts crawling towards me, the way a lion backs its prey into a corner. My eyes are darting across the floor around me, looking desperately for something to defend myself with. I look back at Arie, now at ten feet away.

Frantically, I reach out for a chunk of concrete sitting up against the wall a couple of feet away from me. I meet Arie's eyes, still midnight black, but now at a little over five feet away. She hesitates and then starts crawling faster while letting out that same blood-curdling scream as before and I lunge towards the rock to my right.

Just as I grab it, Arie grabs my calf and digs her nails

in as she makes her way up my body towards my chest. In one swift right hook, I meet the side of my best friend's head with the solid chunk of concrete. The sickening thud sound that her skull lets out makes me shudder at what I had just done.

Almost instantaneously, her body drops on my lap and I lay back, breathing heavily as the reality of the situation sets in. The warmth flowing from the side of her head soaks my jeans and I flip her over onto her back. Her eyes are open and they're still black, the grin still on her face.

Behind me, the old office door makes a creak sound and I turn around to look up at Lydia.

"Well hello, Leo." She says as she slams an old fire poker against the side of my head.

I wake up a few moments later and find myself surrounded by candles on the floor. I try to sit up, but both my hands and feet are tied together behind me.

"Don't bother," Lydia says. "Struggling will only make it worse."

"What is going on? What the fuck did you do to Arie?" Shouting at her only makes me realize just how bad my headache is. The side of my head is throbbing and I feel the blood trickling down the side of my face.

"Easy, Leo. Your language is so vulgar these days. I

guess that's what you can expect when language evolves and emotion does not. People can't express themselves the way they want to, so throwing the occasional "fuck" around helps them feel better."

"Lydia! What did you do to Arie?"

"I was preparing her."

"Preparing her for what?"

"I was preparing her for a higher purpose. She was special, Leo. But you killed her in cold blood. And then you took your own life out of guilt. Or at least- that's what it'll look like to the police." She smiles as she looks down at me.

Looking at the floor around me, I notice lines of some sort and realize I'm in some chalk-looking circle like on the movie, *The Craft*.

"What is this?" I ask, more pissed off than anything.

"You're my sacrifice."

"Your sacrifice? What the hell are you talking about?"

"You asked me how I was able to do all of this. How I was able to keep bringing us all back. Well, you'll see soon enough just how I was able to. I didn't do it alone, either. I had His help." She says, closing her eyes softly and placing her hands together on her chest.

"Are you talking about God?"

"Not God. At least- not the one you're thinking of, Leo. You think your God would allow something like this to happen? No. Most people call Him the devil- maybe you've even heard Him called Lucifer, but He helps people- more than your God does, anyway. Just look at the gift He's given me already. The power of reincarnation is at my fingertips and it's all for the sake of revenge."

"You really did sell your soul, didn't you?" I'm shocked, but at the same time, relieved for some reason.

"I wouldn't say I sold my soul, Leo. I just made a pact to keep making people suffer all for His sake. Arie was going to be the Unholy Vessel for Him to travel around this plane in, but you ruined it. Days of work separating her soul from her body are lost, so now you have to die so I can find a new one. You're a liability and you've only been getting in my way this time around.

"You're insane. You actually believe the words you're saying, don't you?"

"Is it really that hard to believe? You've been remembering your past lives. And what about Arie? You saw her eyes. How do you explain that away? Drugs? Science?" She starts laughing and it makes my blood boil.

"Fuck you." I hiss.

She stops laughing and starts walking towards me, stopping just outside of the circle surrounding me, "No, Leo. Fuck you. You ruined my life and just like every time before, I'm going to ruin yours."

Almost instantly, her eyes go white and she sinks to

her knees with her hands out to her sides, palms facing the ceiling of the mildewy office we're in. The candlelight causes her shadow to bend and twist on the wall behind her. She starts speaking in tongues and her head twitches from side to side.

In a zombie-like manner, Lydia begins to stand herself up and her arms drop to her sides. Then she stiffens and lifts her head; our eyes meeting after returning to their normal state. Lydia looks pissed off now, more than she did a few seconds ago.

"His will is the only way." She says, meeting my surprised expression.

"What just happened?"

"He's chosen a new vessel," She says through gritted teeth.

"A new vessel? Who?" She stares at me emotionless. "Me? Fuck that."

"You don't have a choice, Leo. I owe Him my unwavering servitude for eternity. He owns me. What He wants, He ultimately gets."

"You owe me answers! I don't give a shit what he wants!"

"And I've answered your questions!" She yells back at me. "You wanted to know why I was doing all this- revenge! You wanted to know how- I sold my soul! You've figured it all out, Leo. There's nothing else to say."

The candles start to flicker and it feels like a cold wind

comes across the floor towards me. My vision starts to blur, but I can still make out Lydia's shape standing a little further away from me than she was originally. I feel a tickle start at my feet and it runs up my leg, around my groin, and up my torso to my neck. When it gets to my face, I feel my mouth start to open against my own will and I start choking on my tongue.

My body starts convulsing and I frantically start turning my head this way and that, hoping Lydia will come to my rescue with whatever ounce of humanity she has left in her. It seems to work, because she darts across the room and kicks at the circle drawn on the floor.

Just as quickly as the pain had started, it was gone in a flash and with it, my consciousness.

CHAPTER 24

The rev of an engine wakes me up along with the jerking motion of the car accelerating from a parked position. My eyes adjust pretty quickly- it's nighttime now so it didn't take much. I'm in the back seat, still tied up, too. Lydia is driving and aside from the occasional sound of a car passing by, the ride is silent.

"Where are we?" I manage to mutter out as I use whatever core-strength I have to sit right side up in the back seat. "What happened back there?"

Lydia looks at me through the rearview mirror, "The devil himself happened. Well- almost. I broke the binding circle before the ritual was complete."

"Binding circle? Is that what that chalk shit was?"

She rolls her eyes hard and shakes her head, "It was salt- not chalk. I wasn't drawing a fucking hop-scotch outline. This is serious, Leo."

I sigh, "Listen- I'm sorry. I don't know what you've been through. I can't even imagine it. But this has to stop, Lydia. We can't keep going like this."

"Don't you think I know that now? It's too late. It's His game. I betrayed him and now it'll never stop."

"I need to understand what you're talking about. I know you said you gave him your soul, but what happened back there, exactly? What was that feeling? It didn't hurt at first, but then it felt like I was being ripped apart!" I wince, remembering the pain.

"You were in a binding circle meant for Arie. I offered her body to Him as a sacrifice to use as a vessel. When we left the house that day, Arie and I, she caught on pretty quickly that it was all my fault. I had no choice but to knock her out about ten minutes into the drive. He came to me in a vision and spoke about wanting to walk the Earth again. It just so happened that I had a body readily available- Arie.

So I pulled off the highway at the first vacant-looking stop that I could and performed a disembodiment ritual to separate her spirit from her physical body. It seemed like it was working, but then another entity took over before

He could. That's why she seemed so off- trust me, I know. Although, I have no idea why she didn't attack me like she did you."

"So you killed Arie a long time ago? Is that what you're saying?" I glare at her in the rearview mirror, but she doesn't make eye contact.

"Not necessarily kill, but I made her body an empty shell we'll say. Then He came to me in another vision telling me where to go to perform the correct ritual to remove the inhabiting soul so He could then go inside of her. That's when you came in and fucked it all up. You killed His vessel and He then wanted you as His new vessel." She finally looks at me, and I look away with tear-filled eyes.

I sit in silence for a while, looking out the window at the passing scenery and surprisingly my mind is quiet. I don't know what to say. The crazy thing about it all is that I believe every word. This isn't the strangest night I've had- not by a long shot.

"So what do we do now? How do we end it?"

"Well- and you'll probably love this bit- the only way to break this reincarnation cycle is to kill the person who's responsible for starting it."

"You don't mean-"

"Yes, Leo. You need to kill me."

"I don't want to kill you. I want to stop you!" I protest.

"Unfortunately, the only way to stop me is to kill me."

We drove the rest of the way in silence. I couldn't bear to continue talking about killing Lydia. Regardless of whether or not she deserves it, I don't want to kill someone if I can help it. The last two people were out of defense- that's what I'm telling myself, at least.

"You never answered me, by the way."

"For fuck sake, Leo. What else do you wanna know? I've told you everything. I don't know what else there is to tell!"

"You never told me where we were going."

She breathes out abruptly, "You're right. I didn't. We're going as far away from that warehouse as possible." Her eyes are darting from side to side of the highway, scanning billboards it looks like. "There's a motel coming up on the next exit- let's pull off and rest."

"I think I've gotten enough rest. You had me knocked out cold earlier, remember?"

"We're pulling off to rest," She looks seemingly through me when she looks into the rearview mirror.

I nod and we pull off the exit into the motel's parking lot. When she puts the car in park, she turns and looks at me for a few seconds before pulling out a knife and reaching towards me.

"Lydia, no!"

She pushes me to the side and grabs my hands. I feel her sawing at the ropes and then feel the pop when my hands are free. When I sit up, she's holding the knife hilt-side towards me.

"Cut the rope off your ankles."

I do as I'm told and she continues, "Okay now get out of the car with me and follow my lead."

"What are we doing?" I ask, curious about why she freed my hands and feet.

"We need a room, don't we? So follow my lead."

We walk into the dimly lit office of the motel and the bell above the door rings loudly with a metallic cling as the staff walks from behind old saloon-like doors to the counter before us. She's an older woman with yellowing teeth and more hair on her mustache than I have on my whole body.

"Need a room, lovers?"

Lydia, faking a giggle, says, "Yes, ma'am!" Her cheeks start glowing red.

"One bed or two?" She looks at me.

Too stunned to speak, I open my mouth, but Lydia continues, "Just one is fine. Gotta keep my eye on this little devil!" She gives me a wink and turns back to the concierge who's blushing as she turns to grab a room key.

"Room 34. It's all yours. Payment is due in half right now and balance on check-out." She holds out her hand, palm facing up. "Card or cash?"

"Oh, sweetie, do you mind paying and I'll go get the stuff from the car?" She quickly passes me her credit card and heads towards the front door of the office. When the bell chimes again, I'm left in the office with a Golden Girl and a credit card I'm sure is stolen.

Without checking, I hand the card to the woman and wait for her to charge it. After a few seconds, she hands it back to me and says, "Enjoy your stay!"

My mind flashes back to Adam and how I wish it were him telling me that instead. "Thanks!" I say as I head towards the exit myself.

When I walk outside, Lydia is waving for me to come back to her. As I approach her near her SUV, she hands me one of her bags and we start walking towards Room 34. The rest of the motel looks dark. The only cars in the lot are ours and another that I'm assuming is the office employee's. We're alone here too- great.

Once inside, Lydia locks the deadbolt and pulls the curtains shut. "Okay so we rest here for the night and then continue on our way first thing tomorrow morning. Feel free to sleep in the bed with me, but don't even think of pulling a fast one. I'm a light sleeper. I'll kill you before you have a chance to kill me, Leo."

"Wouldn't dream of it, Lydia." I roll my eyes and head towards the bathroom, "I'm going to shower. Don't wait up." I close the door behind me and turn on the water. It runs cold for the longest time before turning slightly warm.

Eventually it heats up to a comfortable degree and I realize it's all the way on hot. Great- no water pressure and barely any hot water. Fantastic. I undress and step into the shower, which feels slightly worse than the one back at the hotel.

I decide to make do with what I have and continue washing my body. I step into the stream and start washing my face, closing my eyes to avoid getting any soap in them. Only- when I close my eyes, it's as if I'm in a different place and it's full of pain and suffering. People are dying all around me and I'm covered in blood.

I open my eyes too quickly and they start burning when the soap gets in them. I try to rinse them as best I can, but each time I close my eyelids, I see visions of that awful place over and over again. I've had enough of the shower, so I bend down to turn off the faucet and notice the steam rising rapidly from the tub.

Strange, I think to myself. The water feels cool- why's there steam?

Once the last few drops of water fall from the tap, I

grab my towel and begin drying off. After I tie the towel around my waist, I slide the curtain open and can see a blur of myself in the foggy mirror and notice the humidity in the air is thick from the shower. I remove my towel and use it to wipe the mirror above the sink.

With the first swipe, I can see myself, scruffy beard growing in again and messy hair. I wipe my towel in the opposite direction and I freeze when I see someone else with cold, grey-colored eyes staring back at me. I let out a scream and drop to my knees. Building up the courage to stand back up, Lydia begins beating on the bathroom door. Her muffled voice calling my name.

I stand up and keep my eyes facing down, slowly raising them to eye level, weary of who I'm going to see looking back at me. Instead, I see myself in the reflection- this time, however, something looks different about me. I lean in to the mirror to get a better look at my reflection and that's when I notice the difference. One of my eyes is the normal blue; the other a cold, stone-grey.

"Hello, Leo." A voice says from behind me that causes the hair on my body to stand tall. I spin around fast, but there's no one there. Instead, laughter comes from behind me again, so I spin around back to my original position and see the grey-eyed man staring back at me once again. "It's great to finally meet you."

"This isn't real." I say, rubbing my eyes vigorously.

"Oh, but it is, Leo. You're not seeing things. I'm as real as you are."

"Who are you?" I say, in shock. "What do you want from me?"

The man in the mirror chuckles a bit to himself before answering, "Those seem like loaded questions. In due time, Leo. In due time. For now, get some rest. There's a lot we need to go over."

"No- fuck that. I'm tired of waiting for answers. I want to know what's going on and now. Who the fuck are you?"

The man raises his eyebrow, and I feel mine raise as well, "I have many names, Leo. But you can call me whatever you'd like."

I fall silent, unable to speak even if I wanted to.

"And you, my friend, are in my body."

Made in the USA
Middletown, DE
25 March 2023

27640044R00146